My heart was pounding. . . .

The Unicorns had gathered around and were eagerly reading over my shoulder.

"Oh, my God!" Mary shrieked. "It's a love scene."

Phil Silkin, Tom Sanders's assistant, grinned. "Well, sort of. It's a comic romantic scene."

"It's got a kiss in it," Jessica breathed enviously.

My heart was pounding. A love scene? I'd never done a love scene before. Comic or not. Suddenly, my palms were sweaty. What was I going to do?

"Who's the lucky guy that Maria gets to kiss?" Ellen asked, giggling.

"Maria will be playing opposite Brad Marshall," Phil answered.

There was an earsplitting squeal. Brad Marshall was one of the world's hottest teen stars. And major adorable. Skin the color of caramel. Long black lashes. Tall. Athletic. And just about the last person in the world I'd want to play opposite in my first love scene.

THE UNICORN CLUB™

MARIA'S MOVIE COMEBACK

Written by
Alice Nicole Johansson

Created by
FRANCINE PASCAL

BANTAM BOOKS
NEW YORK · TORONTO · LONDON · SYDNEY · AUCKLAND

To Mia Pascal Johansson

RL 4, 008-012

MARIA'S MOVIE COMEBACK
A Bantam Book / February 1994

Sweet Valley High® and The Unicorn Club™
are trademarks of Francine Pascal

Conceived by Francine Pascal

Produced by Daniel Weiss Associates, Inc.
33 West 17th Street
New York, NY 10011

Cover art by James Mathewuse

ISBN: 0-553-48206-8

Published simultaneously in the United States and Canada

Bantam Books are published by Bantam Books, a division of Bantam Doubleday Dell Publishing Group, Inc. Its trademark, consisting of the words "Bantam Books" and the portrayal of a rooster, is Registered in U.S. Patent and Trademark Office and in other countries. Marca Registrada. Bantam Books, 1540 Broadway, New York, New York 10036.

PRINTED IN THE UNITED STATES OF AMERICA

OPM   0 9 8 7 6 5 4 3 2 1

One

Well! All I can say is that if *you* think it's weird that I, Maria Slater, am over at Mandy Miller's house at a meeting of the Unicorn Club, just think how weird *I* must be feeling.

Let's face it—last year, when we were all in the sixth grade, I agreed with Elizabeth Wakefield one hundred percent about the Unicorn Club. We couldn't stand them. We even called them the Snob Squad. Traditionally, they were a club made up of the prettiest and most popular girls at Sweet Valley Middle School—and they never let anybody forget it.

But this year, the club changed. I mean really changed, for the better. Janet Howell, who was the president last year, went on to Sweet Valley High. Janet was a big bossy snob. She started the club, so I guess everybody sort of copied her personality. But now, without her around, the other girls feel freer to be themselves. And you know what? They're all pretty nice. So when they asked me and Elizabeth Wakefield to join, we said yes.

Then we wondered if we'd lost our minds.

I think we were still wondering if we'd lost our minds as we exchanged a look and a secret smile across Mandy Miller's living room. We were having one of our weekly meetings. The Unicorns try to get together at least once a week. And sometimes we have emergency sessions in the middle of the week.

This was one of our regular meetings, though. It was Monday afternoon, and Mandy, our new president, was filling us in on where we stood.

Actually, we were on pretty shaky ground. A few weeks ago—*before I joined* (let's be clear on that point)—the Unicorns hadn't found their new identity and they did some pretty dumb, mean, and destructive things while they were having (get this) a dare war.

That's right. You heard me. A *dare war*. Have you ever heard of anything more ridiculous? And here's the kicker: the dare war was to pick a president for their club. Needless to say, they abandoned this cheese-brained idea when the club got into terrible trouble (more on that in a minute). Finally, they elected Mandy president, mainly because she was the one who seemed to have the right slant on what a club should be. She said a good club is the kind of club that brings out the best in its members and not the worst.

That made a lot of sense to me. So here I am, along with Elizabeth and Mandy and Mary and Ellen and . . .

Oops. I forgot. You might not know everybody.

Now, I know it's boring if you already know everybody in the room to have to listen to everybody get introduced all over again. But some people haven't met the Unicorns before, so I'm going to tell you who they are.

First, holding the green plastic gavel she uses to call our meetings to order, is Mandy. Mandy is a strange combination of good common sense and incredible creativity. You can always talk to her about a problem and get sensible advice. But she's also Sweet Valley Middle School's resident free spirit—at least as far as fashion goes. The rest of us get jealous because she can put together a show-stopping, knock-your-socks-off thrift-store outfit for about three dollars while the rest of us are spending an entire allowance on a pair of jeans.

Mary Wallace, sitting in the chair just to Mandy's left, is somebody I like a lot, too. She's really preppy and she has long blond hair and big gray eyes. Mary is bighearted and can't stand to see anybody get their feelings hurt, and she never says anything bad about anybody.

Next to me on the Millers' big flowered couch is Lila Fowler. Wow! What can I tell you about Lila? She lives like a Beverly Hills movie star. (I know about Beverly Hills movie stars, believe me.) Lila's parents are divorced, and she lives with her dad, who happens to be one of the richest people in town. Lila's very spoiled, but when she gets going on a project or a charity or sees somebody she can help, she'll dig into her pocket and pull out the last dime. No kidding. She comes off kind of snotty, but when you get to know her you find out she's really pretty much of a softy.

Ellen Riteman's kind of hard to read. She's nice enough. Sort of ditsy and funny. And she's a good mimic. She does her mother, who's really overprotective and obnoxious, to a T. I think she's kind of a follower, though. Maybe I just don't know her that well, so I won't say anything more about her.

Now, that brings us to Elizabeth and Jessica Wakefield. They're identical twins. Really. People can't tell them apart. Both of them have shoulder-length blond hair, blue-green eyes, and a dimple in their left cheeks. I guess I should have said *most* people can't tell them apart. But I can. Because Elizabeth Wakefield is my best friend.

Elizabeth is really down-to-earth, a great student, and a good problem solver. Which works out great, because Jessica is out in the ozone and a terrible student— and she creates all kinds of problems. Then Elizabeth and the rest of her friends have to bail her out.

Elizabeth is a pretty good sport about it, though. She's really close to Jessica in spite of the fact that they're totally different. Even though Elizabeth swears this is the year she's going to make Jessica responsible for solving her own problems, she still puts up with a lot more from Jessica than I would put up with from my sister. But then my sister is an older, wiser, mature kind of sister. Her name is Nina, and she's an honors student at Sweet Valley High, where she's in the tenth grade.

Now that you've met the others, allow me to introduce myself. My name is Maria Slater, and up until a couple of years ago, I was known as *the* Maria Slater.

I guess I'd better explain. See, I used to be a child star in Hollywood. I was in a bunch of movies and TV shows. I did commercials, too, most notably for Softee toilet paper and Princess macaroni. The Princess company sold three million boxes of macaroni as soon as the commercial hit the air. *The* Maria Slater was even on the cover of *Folks* magazine—giving its readers what was called "the most winning smile in America."

But by the time I was about to start sixth grade, the parts were few and far between. In fact, I hadn't worked in months. Then my dad was offered a great job in Sweet Valley, California. He's a financial analyst for a big accounting company. My mom visited here and liked what she saw. Sweet Valley Middle School is one of the best in the country. And the town is sort of like a storybook town. Beautiful homes. Well-kept lawns. Nice people. Great shopping. Not to mention gorgeous weather all the time.

I knew Mom, Dad, and Nina were ready to get out of Hollywood. But they let it be my decision. They weren't going to force me out of show business if I wasn't ready. But they also told me that I could always resume my show business career later on. They said it was important to have friends, go to school, be a normal seventh-grader.

I thought about it for a long time. I wasn't a little kid anymore. But I wasn't a big teenager yet, either. In show-business terms, I was at that "awkward age." Hard to cast. A part of me still wanted to be an actress, but I also knew it was time to move on.

So anyway, that's how I wound up living in Sweet

Valley as plain old Maria Slater—just another seventh-grader at Sweet Valley Middle School.

Well, that's everybody. So back to the meeting. I think I mentioned before that the Unicorns were involved in this big dare war. Two things happened during the dare war that the club was still trying to straighten out with Sweet Valley Middle School's resident law-and-order fiend, Mr. Clark—also known as our principal.

You see, Mr. Clark has this toupee. Or he used to. One of the dares was to steal Mr. Clark's toupee and hang it on the door of the cafeteria. Jessica and Lila did it, and in the process, the toupee was ruined. I think it got stepped on or something. Mr. Clark was furious and he put the club on probation. They were sentenced to thirty hours of community service at the Sweet Valley Child Care Center, which provides day care for low-income families. This turned out pretty nicely, because the Unicorns discovered they liked working with the kids at the Center. (P.S.: Elizabeth and I have been volunteering there since sixth grade, but the other Unicorns didn't get into the do-good stuff until this year—when they were sentenced to it.)

The second thing they did during the dare war was paint a purple stripe down the central bank of lockers in the South Hall. Purple is the official color of the Unicorns, so I guess they thought that was funny. Actually, to tell the truth, *they* didn't do it. *Jessica* did. But the others egged her on, so we figured that made the whole club responsible.

It was the locker thing that was on everybody's mind today, because as soon as Mandy got through calling the meeting to order, Jessica stood up.

"As some of you may have heard," she began in a very formal club voice, "Mr. Clark told me today that the Unicorns had better get those lockers that we *vandalized* repainted—*pronto*." Jessica looked around the room and grinned. The whole school had probably heard. Mr. Clark is a pretty nice guy. But even his patience has its limits. I guess walking around bald for the last couple of weeks was really getting on his nerves. And walking into school every morning and seeing that purple stripe probably just sent him over the edge. Finally today, he blew.

"If you girls don't do something about repainting those lockers, I'll expel each and every one of you, and I don't care how many little kids come marching by with picket signs" is what he actually said—no, *shouted*—to Jessica. (The kids from the Center had staged a protest at school to keep the Unicorns from being permanently banned after the dare war pranks.)

"He sounded pretty serious," Jessica said, "and I don't know about you guys, but I don't want to be on probation again. And I sure don't want to be expelled. Any volunteers to help repaint the lockers?"

Every hand, including mine, went up, and Jessica smiled. "Thanks, guys. I'll check with the paint store about paint and prices. I asked Mr. Peters, from the school maintenance department, and he said the color they use on all the metal surfaces is called Industrial Pink."

"You mean that strange no-color beige color they

paint all the lockers is supposed to be pink?" Ellen asked in a tone of disbelief.

"Industrial Pink," Jessica confirmed.

"Now, that's the kind of thing that gives a perfectly good color like pink a bad name," Mandy said in a voice of disgust.

Everybody giggled.

"Anybody want to come with me to the paint store tomorrow to check it out?" Jessica asked.

Again, several hands went up.

"All right. We'll stop at Casey's on the way back and get some ice cream."

Jessica sat down and Mandy stood again. "Now for the big question. How are we going to come up with the money to repay Mr. Clark for his toupee?"

"I don't think we should," Lila said. "He looks better without his toupee."

Everybody applauded. No doubt about it. Once you got used to it, Mr. Clark looked a whole lot better without his toupee.

"That's not the point," Mandy said. "The point is, we damaged property that belonged to him and it's our responsibility to reimburse him."

"How about we treat him to a makeover at the Men's Spa in Beverly Hills," Lila put in, choking on a laugh.

Everybody cracked up, but then Mandy banged her little green plastic gavel on the coffee table. "Order! Order!" Then she blushed and grinned as we all settled down, as though she felt kind of silly being so authoritarian. "Seriously, folks, does anybody have any money-making ideas?"

"A car wash?" Mary suggested.

"They just opened a new one on Elm Street," Elizabeth said. "And it's really cheap. My father says it's the best deal in town."

"Bake sale?" Jessica suggested.

"Who knows how to bake?" Mandy asked, looking out across the room.

Only one hand went up—Elizabeth's. Most of us can cook up spaghetti or pork chops if we have to, but baking cakes and pies is beyond our culinary capabilities.

There was a long pause while we all racked our brains trying to think of something. Finally, Mandy cleared her throat. "I have an idea."

We all sat forward.

Mandy plucked at the baggy canvas pants she wore. On top, she had on a ribbed T-shirt, and over that a string vest. And on her head she wore something that looked like a Smurf hat. I don't know too many people who could carry off a look like that, but Mandy can.

"As you all know," she said, "I'm sort of a thrift-store fan."

"Well, duh!" Mary giggled.

Mandy grinned. "There's a new one on the corner of Rice and Mill streets, called the Attic. They've got clothes, jewelry, furniture, dishes, toys—everything. The lady who owns it is going to be out of town for two weeks. Her niece can run the shop until three thirty, but then she has to go home and take care of her kids. So the owner wants two people to help out and keep the shop open from three thirty to six thirty."

"Are you saying we should get her to hire us?" I asked.

Mandy nodded. "I think it would be fun. And it'll give us a chance to make a little money. Who wants to volunteer to go with me tomorrow to talk to the owner?"

Before I knew it, my hand shot up. I guess this club stuff was getting to me. But I wanted to be involved. And this sounded like fun.

"Great!" Mandy grinned at me. "We'll meet after school tomorrow and walk over there together."

She looked around at everybody and grinned. "Anything else we need to talk about?"

Nobody said anything.

Mandy hit the coffee table with the plastic gavel. "Meeting adjourned. Let's eat some cookies."

After the meeting, I walked back over to the Wakefields' house with Elizabeth, and we went up to her room to hang out for a while before I had to go home to dinner.

"So what did you think of the meeting?" Elizabeth asked with a grin. "Think we did the right thing by joining?"

"I think so. So far, I'm having fun. I like all the girls. And they seem to be really interested in the same things we are: the day-care center, school, arts, fashion, books, extracurricular activities . . . speaking of which," I added breathlessly, "I auditioned this morning for the lead in the drama club's new play."

Elizabeth grabbed a notebook from her desk and ran over to my side, like a frantic reporter. "Miss Slater!

Miss Slater! Can I get an interview with the star of the Sweet Valley Middle School drama department?"

I laughed. Like me, Elizabeth wants to be a writer or a journalist when she grows up. Last year, she was the editor-in-chief of *The Sixers,* the official sixth-grade newspaper. But this year, she's a reporter on the *7 & 8 Gazette.*

I laughed and struck a Hollywood pose. Then I crossed my eyes and stuck out my front teeth. "Why, sure. And why don't you get a few pictures while you're at it?"

Before I knew it, she did exactly that—grabbed her camera and got a shot of that horrible face before I could stop her.

"Some friend you are," I scolded.

Elizabeth laughed. "Someday, when you're really famous, I'll send that picture to the *National Movie Tabloid.*"

We both laughed, but then I got serious. "I may not ever be a famous movie star," I said. "I may not even get the lead in the school play."

Elizabeth rolled her eyes. "Don't be a dope. Of course you will. You're the only one in the department with any professional experience. You've got to be better than anybody else who tried out. The part's yours. You know it is."

I did know it. Deep down, I just knew it. Of course I'd get the part. I was Maria Slater. *The* Maria Slater. Why was I being so silly? I guess because no matter how sure I was, there was still that last little bit of lingering doubt that you always have about a "sure thing."

"Speaking of show biz," Elizabeth said, "I saved this." She reached under a pile of things on her desk and pulled out a newspaper. She opened it up to the "Around Town" section and put her finger on a little item. "'Independent filmmaker Tom Sanders plans to shoot new movie in Sweet Valley,'" she read out loud.

"What do you know," I mused. "We're getting almost as show-biz as Hollywood. I wonder if the people who did that horror movie here last year had anything to do with it? The director of that movie might have had some nice things to say about the town."

Elizabeth grinned. "Hard to imagine, since it turned out to be a real live ghost story—and his star turned out to be a real live monster."

"Shawn Brockaway!" we both said together, and then we made gagging noises.

If ever there was a posturing, demanding, spoiled, sulking teen star, it was Shawn Brockaway. When she was here, she was just horrible to everybody.

I shrugged. "Let's face it. Sweet Valley is a great shooting location. Not much traffic in the streets. Lots of teen hangouts. And Tom Sanders is famous for his comic teen romances."

"Really," Elizabeth said. "I didn't know that."

"Oh, yeah," I said. "He's really famous. But really eccentric, from what I've read. He always shoots with an amazingly low budget. He likes funky-looking people and sets. And he always tries to keep it fun."

"He sounds nice."

I grinned. "Maybe someday I'll get to work with

him. In the meantime, I'll settle for the lead in the school play."

Elizabeth picked up her pillow and walloped me on the head. "Quit being silly. You know you'll get the part. You just know you will."

I grabbed the pillow and whacked her back. But I didn't say anything. What was there to say? She was right. Absolutely, positively, no-doubt-about-it right. (I hoped.)

Two

The next day was Tuesday, and right on schedule Mandy met me on the front school steps as soon as classes were over.

Both of us carried backpacks, and I noticed Mandy's had a whole bunch of buttons all over it—political buttons from the fifties, sixties, and seventies. Cartoon buttons. Buttons with sayings on them. Buttons with movie stars on them.

It was really funky and eye-catching. Exactly the kind of thing Mandy always comes up with.

"Great buttons," I said, laughing when I saw one of myself at about age four promoting a TV movie.

"I got them at the Attic. They have a whole bin full of them. Have you been there yet?" Mandy asked me as we passed the card shop and the bakery.

I shook my head. "Not yet."

"It's incredible," Mandy said. Her eyes were getting that bright glow they always get when she talks about thrift stores and clothes. "The Attic isn't as big as the Clothes Closet," she was saying as we walked down the street. (The Clothes Closet is Sweet Valley's other big thrift store). "But I think the things in the Attic are cooler. More vintage, if you know what I mean. And the lady who runs it is major cool. You're really going to like her. She's Asian. About my grandmother's age. And she has this long straight hair down to her waist with a lot of gray in it. I just love the way she dresses. Total vintage sophistication."

I didn't say anything, but it was weird. The woman she was describing reminded me of someone I had known in Hollywood. Her name was Clara Kim and she was a huge movie star. But there were probably a lot of women who would fit that physical description.

Pretty soon, we were outside the door of the Attic. Mandy pushed the door open and we walked in. The place had a funky, musty smell, and on the racks I saw all kinds of secondhand clothes. There were knickknacks and lamps and furniture, too. And the strangest thing is, it all gave me a weird sense of déjà vu. I had the feeling I'd seen a lot of this stuff before. The furniture. The lamps. A lot of the knickknacks.

A lady stepped forward from the shadows in the back of the shop. "May I help you?" she asked in a pleasant voice.

Then she took a good look at me, and I took a good look at her, and the next thing we knew, we were shrieking with laughter and hugging each other.

"Clara! What are you doing here?"

"What are *you* doing here?" she demanded.

"I take it you two know each other?" Mandy asked with a grin.

Both of us began to laugh. "I've known this one since she was in diapers," Clara answered. "In fact, I met Maria when we were filming a diaper commercial." She ran a hand over my hair. "And look how tall you are. You're practically all grown up."

I grinned. "That's sort of what I'm doing here. It's hard to be a child star when you're over five feet tall. So I decided to take a break for a while. Go to school. Make some friends. Then maybe go back to Hollywood. What about you?"

Clara smiled and shrugged. "I'm taking a break, too. But not by choice. The telephone just doesn't ring very often anymore," she said with a rueful smile. "So now I'm trying to make a living in the thrift-store business."

"But you were a big star," I protested. "People were always offering you roles."

Clara put her elegant hand on my sleeve. "Times change. I'm older now, Maria. And"—she smiled and motioned to her face—"there aren't many parts for *mature* women." She laughed.

Her face was still beautiful to me. I was just about to tell her how unfair it was that something as natural as getting older would hurt her career, when she waved her hand and changed the subject. "Tell me, are you at Sweet Valley Middle School?"

I nodded. "We both are," I said, nudging Mandy.

"Then maybe you've seen my granddaughter, Evie Kim. She's in the sixth grade. She moved here with me. You remember Evie?"

I smacked my hand against my forehead. "Of course. I kept noticing a girl staring at me the last few days and I thought she looked familiar. But I just couldn't place her."

I turned to Mandy. "Clara and I were in a TV movie together a few summers ago, and Evie came to the set every day with Clara," I explained. "We got to be good friends for a while, and I visited her at Clara's house sometimes on weekends."

Then a light bulb went off in my head suddenly. I knew why so much of the stuff in the shop looked familiar. They were the things out of Clara's house. There was the camelback sofa that had been in the front hall. And over it hung the painting of the canals of Venice that had been in Clara's dining room. My eyes flew around the store, recognizing lamps and chairs and decorative objects.

Something strange was going on here. And I had a feeling I knew what. But I couldn't think of any tactful way to ask. Besides, we were talking about Evie right now.

I turned back to Clara. "Why didn't she say hello or tell me who she was?"

"Because I didn't think you remembered me," said a shy voice in the doorway.

We all turned and saw Evie standing in the doorway with her backpack, carrying a violin case.

"Not remember you!" I cried, hurrying forward to give her a hug. "How could I forget you? My shadow. I just didn't *recognize* you without the pigtails."

Evie laughed and shook her head, making her long, straight black hair ripple like a curtain. The last

time I saw her, she had worn her hair in two tight
pigtails on the sides of her head. Plus, she had been a
little kid—in little kids' clothes. Now, in her sleek
jeans and turtleneck, she looked grown-up, sophisticated.

Clara laughed. "We called her Maria's shadow because Evie used to follow Maria around everywhere,"
she explained to Mandy. "She adored Maria and
thought she was the most wonderful person in the
whole world."

Evie was blushing. "Oh, Grandma," she said
softly. "I'm sure I was a big pest."

I put my arm around her. "Are you kidding? You
could never be a pest." I smiled. "I hope we'll be
friends again now that you've moved here."

Evie smiled shyly and seemed pleased. It was
strange seeing Evie act shy. She had always moved
and talked at the speed of light. But now everything
in her life had changed. New town. New school. New
everything. I guessed she was feeling confused about
a lot of things. It was going to take her a while to feel
like her old self again.

It was strange, but back when we were kids, the
one-year age difference between us had seemed huge.
I always felt as if I was the big kid and Evie was the
little kid. But now that we were in middle school, it
didn't make so much difference. We were practically
the same age, and I felt sure we had a lot in common.

"Still playing the violin?" I pointed to the case.

Clara smiled. "She's a genius with the violin.
That's why we came to Sweet Valley. I couldn't afford
to keep her in the private music school in Beverly

Hills anymore. In fact," she added with a laugh, "I couldn't afford our house anymore. So we moved here. There's an excellent teacher here in Sweet Valley. And my sister lives here. We're staying with her for now until we get a little money tucked away." She glanced at her watch. "Speaking of lessons, Evie, it's time for you to go."

Evi glanced at the clock on the wall, and her eyes widened slightly. "Gosh. I'm even running a little late." She threw her backpack behind the counter, kissed Clara on the cheek, and fluttered her fingers at me and Mandy. "See you guys tomorrow at school," she said.

"See you," we both chorused.

Clara watched her go with a fond and proud smile. "Evie will be in and out of the shop in the afternoons," she said. "But she takes several lessons and practices every day. That has to come first. Always. The violin comes first. She's good, Maria. Concert career material. "

Clara had been so matter-of-fact about their troubles, it had seemed inappropriate to make any kind of sympathetic remarks. So I nodded and tried to smile, as if I were happy about everything Clara was telling me. But I really felt sad. Clara seemed cheerful and positive, but it was obvious that she was having really hard times, and my heart was just breaking for her. Actors have a lot of pride. And they hate admitting that things aren't going well. Especially after they've been on top.

When I knew Clara in Hollywood, she had everything. Now it looked as though it was all gone.

Everything that went with the movie-star life: the jewelry, the clothes, the houses, the glamour, and the fans. Even her furniture was sitting in a thrift shop, ready to be sold.

Well, she wasn't the first. And she wouldn't be the last. I guess most people would shrug and say, "That's show business" or "Whoever said life is fair?" But it's just like anything else that's sad or unfair—it seems even sadder and more unfair when it happens to somebody you actually know and care about.

I hoped I could figure out some way to help her. Then I had a horrible thought and a shiver went down my spine. Maybe I would need somebody to help *me* one day.

"So what do you think, Maria?" I heard Mandy asking me.

"Huh?" I blinked. I'd been so immersed in my own thoughts, I hadn't been listening to the conversation.

Mandy grinned. "We've been talking about the shop while you've been daydreaming. Clara says her niece can run the shop until three thirty every afternoon. But then she has to go home to be with her kids. She lives just next door, so if we need her, she can be here in a minute. But somebody needs to be here in the shop from three thirty to six thirty."

"I want two girls for each afternoon," Clara said with a frown. "Mandy, you said something about a club, and I want to be sure the two of you are going to be the ones in charge here."

Mandy looked at me. "At least one of us will be sure to be here at all times. But the others might come by and help out. Is that OK?"

Clara looked at me. "Maria, can these girls be trusted not to turn the shop into an after-school hangout and make a mess out of things?"

I took a long moment to answer. A few weeks ago I would have said, *Not in a million years*. But things were different now. The Unicorns were girls you could count on. "Absolutely," I said.

Clara smiled. "Fine, then. I'll rely on you girls to use your judgment about how to run things in the afternoons. I'm happy with the arrangements if you're happy."

I nodded. "It's a deal. But where are you going to be?"

Clara waved a hand vaguely. "I'm going to New York to talk with some producers, plus see my agent. It should take a couple of weeks at the most. And I'll leave phone numbers with my sister and my niece and Evie in case of emergency." She waved a hand in the direction of the main part of the store. "Come on. I'll show you what to do."

Over the next hour, Clara showed us around the shop. She showed us how to keep track of the inventory. How to operate the cash register. How she liked the merchandise arranged.

It was all pretty interesting. And Mandy was having a ball looking at all the old hats and shoes and stuff. Turned out lots of the clothes were Clara's old clothes. Some of them had even been movie costumes from the forties, fifties, and sixties.

We left, promising to be there day after tomorrow promptly at three thirty. Clara gave me a big hug, then gave Mandy one for good measure. Then she showed us how to lock up.

By the time we left, it was after five. Mandy had to go home, but as usual, I just had to drop by Elizabeth's and fill her in on everything. Besides, I knew that Jessica and her paint crew had gone by the paint store that afternoon and I wondered if they'd figured out everything they were going to need.

Elizabeth was waiting for me in her room. She was sitting at her desk with her pencil and her calculator, looking sort of like an accountant. Since she gets the best math grades of anybody in the Unicorn Club (anybody in the school, for that matter), she had sort of been made the unofficial club treasurer.

Believe it or not, she was wearing her ponytail tied with a purple ribbon. *Purple!*

I didn't even have to say anything. I just pointed to it and we both started laughing.

Elizabeth's trademark had always been the *blue* ribbon in her ponytail. But purple was the official color of the Unicorn Club. Last year, when we were both in the sixth grade, we would have been dragged over hot coals by wild horses before we would have worn anything purple. OK, that's an exaggeration. But we were definitely *not* big fans of the club.

Times change, though, and so do people. And if purple was good enough for Elizabeth, it was good enough for me. I made a mental note to stock up on purple clothes and accessories, then I told Elizabeth all about Clara and her granddaughter, Evie. Elizabeth said she'd seen her around school, and we both decided to make a point of befriending her as soon as possible. It's tough to be a new kid at school. Take it from me. I know.

Then I told her about the thrift-shop job and how much Clara was going to pay us. Elizabeth frowned, then began adding and subtracting like mad on her calculator. Then she *tsk*ed and sighed. "That doesn't even come close to making enough money to pay Mr. Clark for his toupee. We'll be lucky if it covers the paint for the lockers."

"Speaking of paint, have you heard from the paint crew?"

Elizabeth glanced at her watch. "They should be back any minute. They went to the paint store two hours ago with the locker measurements to see how much paint and what kind of equipment to buy. But I think they were planning to stop at Casey's afterward, so who knows?"

Since Elizabeth and I had not been members of the club when the purple stripe had been painted, everybody had later agreed that we didn't really have any responsibility for repainting the lockers. So Elizabeth had opted to confine her participation to financial consulting, and I decided to work off my part of the debt in the thrift store.

Come to think of it, we didn't have any obligation to repay Mr. Clark, either. But working in the thrift store was going to be fun. It would mainly be me and Mandy. And I hoped Elizabeth would spend a lot of time there. With them I knew I'd have fun—especially in a funky, fun store that was more like a costume shop than anything else.

Just then, there was a lot of banging and laughing

and we heard a bunch of footsteps on the stairs. The next thing we knew, the rest of the Unicorns were piling into Elizabeth's room.

Jessica was all decked out in a pair of new painter's coveralls. She usually wore her long blond hair in loose waves. But today they were sticking out of the back of a painter's cap.

Behind her were Mary Wallace, Ellen Riteman, and Lila Fowler.

"Did you buy any paint?" Elizabeth asked.

"No," Jessica answered. "They have to special mix Industrial Pink. But I put in an order for five cans. It'll be ready in a few days, and the guy will call and tell us when we can pick it up. We all chipped in to cover the deposit, and I spent half my allowance on these coveralls. Don't you think they're cool-looking? And when they get spattered with paint, they'll *really* look cool."

Elizabeth rolled her eyes. "Could we skip the fashion report and cut to the chase? What did you guys find out about the paint? What's the bottom-line price for paint and equipment?"

Mary flopped on her stomach across Elizabeth's bed and told her how much it was going to cost.

Elizabeth groaned and rubbed her hand down her face in frustration.

Jessica ran over and hung over her shoulder. "Come on, Lizzie. You'll figure it out. Just juggle some numbers and we'll find the money." Then she grinned. "Want to know what else I found out about paint?"

"What?" Elizabeth groaned.

"That it comes in about five million colors," Jessica said, laughing.

"She's not exaggerating," Ellen agreed. Jessica reached into her pocket and pulled out a handful of brightly colored pieces of paper that looked like bookmarks. She threw them up in the air like confetti. "Look at all these colors."

Then she reached into her other pocket and pulled out another handful of color samples. So did Ellen and Lila and Mary, and soon they were all throwing them in the air and screaming and laughing.

Within seconds, the floor was covered with bright pieces of paper, and it looked more like we were having a party than an impromptu business meeting. It felt more like a party, too.

"Do you think painting the lockers is going to be hard?" Ellen asked. "I've never painted anything so big before."

"Nahhh," Jessica assured her. "Not with me in charge. It'll probably take us one hour. Max. It'll be a snap. All we have to do is pick up the paint and the equipment, meet at school early one morning, and paint the lockers. We'll do it soon, and then Mr. Clark will be happy."

We sat down on the floor, and the Unicorn Club spent the next hour pawing through the slips and happily arguing over what color we would paint the lockers if we didn't have to paint them Industrial Pink.

We had so much fun that I only barely got home in time for dinner. Made it in just under the wire, though. They were just sitting down when I slipped in the back door, through the kitchen door, into the dining room, and into my chair, giving them my best "Who me, *late*?" look.

Nina was mad because it had been my turn to set the table and she had had to do it because I wasn't home. But then everybody forgot to be mad when I told them about Clara and Evie. Of course, they all remembered them from the old days and had about a zillion questions, most of which I couldn't answer. Mom said as soon as Clara got back from New York, we'd have her and Evie over to dinner.

That suited me fine. It looked as though it was about time somebody did something nice for them.

Three

The next afternoon, Mandy, Elizabeth, and I went over to the Sweet Valley Child Care Center along with Jessica and Mary. At least two of us volunteer there three times a week. And lots of times, everybody comes and lends a hand. Mandy and I were there to explain to Mrs. Willard, the director, that we'd be taking a couple of weeks off for another project, but we were still committed to the Center.

The Center is run by the Sweet Valley Community Services Organization, a nonprofit organization that oversees a number of projects for people who are in trouble or in need. It runs shelters and rehab centers and provides counseling and all kinds of social services. Most of the families of the kids who come to the Center are working or looking for work. None of them have much money, and without the center they wouldn't have any day care at all. So whenever I spend an afternoon there, I feel that I'm doing something really worthwhile.

By the way, this is the place where the Unicorns were "sentenced" to work for thirty hours when they got in trouble with Mr. Clark. Didn't turn out to be much of a punishment, though, since they wound up falling in love with the kids and vice versa.

The Child Care Center itself is sort of run-down and in need of a lot of repairs. Since they're nonprofit, they're always short on money. As we all walked up the broken brick front walk, I began to get that excited feeling I always get when we're about to see the kids.

I love Oliver Washington. He's black, like me, and he's a real handful. He's been at the Center the longest, so he has this idea that he's sort of in charge of the place. But the real light of his life is Jessica. The two of them have a very special bond—Jessica is kind of like his big sister.

There's also Ellie McMillan, who looks like a tiny doll. Her mom is single and works for Lila's dad. Lila and Ellie adore each other.

There's a group of kids we call the Wild Bunch: Arthur Foo is Asian and has about twenty brothers and sisters. They all work at the family green-grocery when they're not in school.

There's also Yuky, who's Korean-American. Then there are the twins—Allison and Sandy Meyer. We call them the Terrible Twosome because they're always fighting.

And there's a bunch of toddlers who come on a semiregular basis, plus occasionally some infants.

For the kids who come there, the center is sort of

like home, and I think all of us feel proud to be a part of it. But today when we walked in, it looked like a bomb had fallen on the place. The middle of the roof in the main hallway had collapsed, and people were running in every direction. Plaster dust was floating in the air. There was debris covering every surface. And puddles of dirty water dotted the hallway.

Mrs. Willard was busy telling everybody what to do. She was shouting directions and telling the other staff members to get on the phone and call the kids' parents.

"What happened?" Elizabeth demanded as a secretary raced past us toward her office.

Mrs. Willard shook her head regretfully. "The roof finally went. It's needed repairing for a long time. All the heavy rains we've had lately finally put too much of a strain on it and it collapsed. We're just lucky no one was injured."

"Mrs. Willard," a woman called out from one of the offices, "what do you want me to tell the parents?"

"Tell them to come immediately and pick the kids up," Mrs. Willard said. "By law, we can't keep them here under these conditions."

She looked at us. "As you all know, the laws governing day-care centers are very stringent. A collapsed roof definitely doesn't meet their specifications."

"How long will it take to fix it?" Mary asked.

"Probably just a couple of days," Mrs. Willard responded in a distracted tone, reaching out to grab Arthur Foo just before he tripped over a pile of rubble. She turned him back in the direction of the playroom where the kids usually hung out, and patted him on the seat. "Go back over there, Arthur."

"So it's really no big problem then," Mandy said in a relieved voice. "The Center will be back to normal in a few days."

Mrs. Willard pushed a pencil through the bun at the back of her head and sighed heavily. "I'm afraid not, girls. It's not time that's the problem. It's money. Over the last month I've gotten three estimates of what it'll cost to replace that roof, and our budget can't even come close to covering it."

She named a figure, and Mary's face fell, as if she absolutely couldn't believe it.

"You mean : . ."

Mrs. Willard nodded grimly. "That's right. It means we're out of business. At least until we can pay for a new roof. And I don't see that happening anytime soon."

Before any of us could say another word, some of the parents began arriving. When they saw the debris in the hall and the hole in the roof, they all looked pretty blown away. And when they realized they wouldn't be able to leave their kids at the Center for a while, they looked devastated.

"But there is no one at home to look after Arthur," Mrs. Foo said sadly in her broken English. Her oldest son, Franklin, stood beside her. "It takes both me and my husband to keep the business running. If I can't bring Arthur here, it means Franklin must stay home from school in order to baby-sit Arthur. He is in college and it is a shame, but he is the only child over sixteen." Mrs. Foo turned to Mrs. Willard. "That is the law. Right? Children under sixteen must attend school. It is mandatory?"

Mrs. Willard nodded.

"Then Franklin must stay home," Mrs. Foo repeated sadly in a bewildered voice. It was clear she desperately wished she could think of another solution.

"Mom!" Franklin protested. "I can't. You know I can't. I have exams and lectures and—" Then he broke off quickly. "Don't worry about it," he said in a low voice when he saw the anguished look on his mother's face. "I'll do it."

Mrs. Foo looked heartbroken. "Franklin is at the top of his class," she explained to me. "And exams are coming up. This is a terrible time for him to miss his classes."

Franklin put his arm around his mom, and then he lifted little Arthur with his other arm. "Don't worry about it," he repeated, obviously forcing his voice to sound cheerful. "Someone will tape my lectures for me. Someone else will take notes. We'll make it work." He shook Arthur playfully. "Right, little one?"

Franklin met my eyes. I could see the pain in them and I realized how much the Center meant to the Foo family. It meant Mr. and Mrs. Foo had a chance to make a living and a life for themselves in America. And it meant Franklin had a chance to get an education and go as far as he wanted in life.

Now all their careful plans were being ruined. All because we didn't have enough money to build a roof.

As I watched them walk away, I admired their spirit, their willingness to work hard, and their unselfish ability to pull together as a family. Surely a family like that deserved all the help a community could give them. Was a day-care center really so much to ask?

"I just sent Ellie home with Mrs. McMillan," Mandy said a little later. "Boy, was she upset!"

"Why?" Jessica asked.

"Because she just spent six months looking for a job. She finally finds one, and now, almost as soon as she starts, she's going to have to call in and say she can't come in for a few days because she doesn't have anyone to care for Ellie. She's worried it'll make her look bad at the office. Maybe even get her fired. She's too new at the job to qualify for any vacation days or family leave."

"Hoo, boy!" I sighed.

Finally, all the kids were packed up with their parents and sent home. And with everyone it was the same story. One mom said she and her husband were going to have to empty their savings to get a baby-sitter. Another set of parents said the father would have to take a leave of absence from his job. And a single mom said she might as well even give up looking for work now. She couldn't take her child along with her on job interviews.

"This is terrible," Jessica said, biting a nail.

"It really is," Mandy said. "I never realized before how many families depend on day care to survive."

Just then, Mrs. Willard came up to us. "As always, girls, we appreciate your help. But you might as well go on home."

"When do you want us to come back?"

I swear, it looked as if Mrs. Willard was going to cry. She shrugged. "I guess we'll just have to call you when we're up and running again. And I'm afraid that's not going to be for a while."

The next day was Thursday—our first day at the thrift shop. And by the time Mandy and I got there, I was feeling pretty low. I did my best to smile, but it wasn't working. I just couldn't stop thinking about what a hard time all those families had probably been having all day.

"Hey!" Mandy said, nudging me in the ribs with her elbow. "Part of mental health is figuring out which problems you can solve and which ones you can't. We can't solve the problems at the Center. At least not now. Not today. So let's concentrate on being here, doing a good job, and having fun doing it."

See what I mean about Mandy? She was exactly right. And the best thing I could have done was put the Center out of my mind for the moment. But for some reason, I just couldn't get the picture of Franklin Foo's disappointed face out of my mind. "You're right. And I'll try. But right now I'm a little down, and I'm having a hard time getting over it."

Mandy pulled a top hat off the rack and stuck it down on top of my head. "Then you're in the right place." She grinned. "Because when I'm feeling down, I get myself dressed *up*. And *zoom*! There go my spirits."

Mandy took me by the shoulders and shoved me toward the clothing racks. She looked me up and

down, tapped her finger against her cheek, and let
out a long and professional-sounding *hmmmm*.

"What are you doing?" I asked uneasily. I wasn't
sure I liked the look in her eye.

"Trust me," she said between giggles, reaching for
a feather boa.

Mandy and I were both laughing so hard we could
hardly stand up straight. Luckily for us, there hadn't
been any customers. Mandy had spent the last half
hour outfitting us both in the funkiest-looking thrift-
store-chic clothes you can imagine.

Like I said before, Mandy has a real flair for that
kind of thing. And she put together combinations
that would never have occurred to me. Like sweat-
pants cut off at the knee worn with a beaded evening
sweater, Lurex stockings, and laced-up ankle boots.

It sounds horrible, and if my mother saw it, she'd
probably have a heart attack. But trust me, if you saw
it at school, you'd be dying for it.

Mandy had herself done up in a sort of twenties-
meets-the-nineties cyberpunk-flapper look. She wore
a straight, short sheath with layers of fringe made out
of strips of metallic fabric. She twisted an old metal-
scrap belt into a twenties-style headband that fit
across her forehead, and finished off the whole en-
semble with seamed stockings and clogs.

We were having so much fun and so many laughs
that I actually forgot the Center for the moment. We
both struck a pose in front of the mirror and then we
jumped about ten feet in the air when we heard a big
burst of giggles explode behind us.

We turned around and saw all the Unicorns gathered there, applauding.

"Fantastic!" Jessica screamed, and Mary whistled her approval between her teeth.

Mandy and I began to strut up and down the shop floor like models, laughing and goofing around. We had just glided past the front door when we had to jump back as somebody shoved it open.

Mandy and I both gasped. Standing there was this really hip-looking guy. He had on a leather jacket and an earring, and his hair was slicked back in a ponytail.

He held up his hands, formed a frame, and squinted at us through it. "Perfect! Unbelievably perfect!"

Mandy and I exchanged an uncomfortable look. After all, it was our first day working in the shop, and this guy was acting kind of strange.

"Can I help you?" Mandy asked in a shaking voice.

The guy looked her up and down, then he looked all around the shop. "I think so. I'm Tom Sanders." He held out his hand to shake hers, then mine. He started talking again. "I'm an independent movie producer and I'm here in Sweet Valley to shoot a teen movie called *Secondhand Rose.*"

"We've heard about you," Mandy said quickly. "They wrote an article about you in the paper."

By this time, the others had gotten the gist of the conversation and were moving in closer for a better look and a better listen.

"Great." Mr. Sanders grinned. "Publicity is always good. But did they also write that this is a very low-budget picture? We're trying to keep the costs down, and since the theme is recycling and funky thrift-store chic, we want to do all the costumes using local thrift-store stuff." He pointed to us. "The way you two girls look is perfect. Just perfect. Exactly the look and mood I'm trying to create."

I put my hand on Mandy's shoulder. "Mandy put our outfits together," I said quickly. "She's a genius when it comes to fashion. She wants to be a costume designer someday. If that sounds like a hint, it is. I know she'd love to help out with the costumes."

(Nobody has ever accused me of being shy. If I want somebody to know something, I tell them.)

Tom Sanders was grinning. Nodding and listening. But he only seemed to be half listening. Mostly he was staring at me. Staring hard.

When I finished talking he slapped his hand against his thigh. *"Maria Slater!* That's who you are. I've been trying to figure it out since I walked in." He grabbed my hand and shook it in both of his. "I've been a fan of yours since your first commercial."

When he said that, it made me feel a burst of pride. I know I said I was enjoying being away from the hype and bustle of professional show business, but just the same, it was nice to be remembered.

"What are you doing these days?" he asked.

I shrugged. "Mostly going to school and being a typical seventh-grader."

He looked me up and down and grinned. "Seventh-grader, yes. Typical, no." Then he looked around and gave everybody a big grin. "Who are your friends?"

It was what everybody had been waiting for. I performed the introductions, and the Unicorns made it pretty clear that they were Tom Sanders Fan Club members.

"I loved *Teen Magic*," Mary breathed.

"My favorite is *Prom Secret*," Ellen squeaked.

Everybody talked for a few more minutes about his movies, and he was really, really nice about listening to everybody's opinion and answering questions.

After a little while, they got around to the subject of his new movie.

"It's going to be great," he said. "Funny. Funky. Romantic. And really off the wall." He gave me a long look. "There's a small part that I haven't cast yet. It would be perfect for you, Maria."

Mandy gasped and Jessica squealed.

Tom held up his hands, telling us all to contain our enthusiasm. "It's a small part, and I know you're used to leading roles. But it's a nice little part. A good character role. And if it's done right, it's going to get some young actress a lot of attention."

"Maria will do it right," Jessica said confidently. "Maria Slater is one of the best actresses in the business—young or old. Right, gang?"

"Right!" They all echoed.

I shook my head. "I don't know," I began. "I've been out of the business for . . ."

"I'll pay you double scale," he said quickly.

Suddenly dollars, cents, and light bulbs appeared in my head. But would double scale be enough? "Make it triple scale and you've got a deal," I said, my heart thumping. Was that really me haggling like an agent? But what the heck? Why not go for it? After all, I was *the* Maria Slater.

He hesitated for just a second, then he held out his hand. "It's a deal. I'll do it on a handshake if you will."

I shook Tom's hand and then turned to the group. "I think I just figured out how we're going to pay for the new roof at the Center."

There was a stunned silence while this sank in.

Then, the next thing I knew, Jessica threw herself into my arms and everybody was hugging me.

"You're the greatest, Maria, the absolute greatest."

Their praise meant a lot. But mostly, I saw Franklin Foo's face. He'd be able to go back to school. And it was like my dad was always telling me: show business is great—but school is the most important job a kid will ever have.

Four

Tom Sanders left late that afternoon after spending a lot of time shooting the breeze and talking movies with the Unicorns. He said he would be driving back and forth between Sweet Valley and Hollywood a lot over the next week, but he gave me about a zillion phone numbers where he could be reached if necessary, as well as the number of his assistant, who was staying in Sweet Valley to help scout locations. Tom wanted my number and Mandy's and Elizabeth's number, too—in case he had to reach somebody in Sweet Valley and couldn't get his assistant.

The shoot was scheduled for a week from Monday, and he said he'd get a copy of the script to me well in advance. He'd have to let me know later where and when we'd do the scene because they hadn't picked a location yet. It would be somewhere in Sweet Valley, though, he promised. The trucks and crew would come to Sweet Valley on the Friday before, and they would be shooting outside scenes around the area all that weekend. Monday would be their final day of shooting here, after which they'd go back to Hollywood to do the remaining scenes in a studio.

Finally, we had all the details straightened out and he was gone. We all just had time for one long group squeal of excitement before closing up the shop for the day. So we made the most of it, and then we cleared out.

I wasn't sure how my folks were going to feel about my accepting the role in the movie. After all, we'd come to Sweet Valley so I could take a break from acting. So I didn't say anything right away when I got home.

I didn't say anything as we sat down to dinner, either.

The main course didn't seem to offer the appropriate atmosphere in which to make such an important announcement. And everybody seemed so happy over dessert, I hated to bring up something that might spoil it for them.

Finally, while my folks were having their coffee, I decided to break the big news. I started out by telling them about the roof at the Center and how all those kids and parents were going to have such a hard time.

"That's terrible," my mother said. She turned to my father. "Jack, you're an accountant. Can't you go over there and look at the Center's books and figure out how they can pay for a roof?"

"First of all," my father said in his stuffy, offended

voice, "I am *not* an accountant. I am a financial analyst. Secondly, that organization has a very competent
accountant. George Greene is a great guy; I've known
him for years. The Center's problem is not that they
don't have an accountant. The Center's problem is
that they don't have enough money. It takes money to
build a roof. If we want to help, I think we're just
going to have to start the usual fund-drive efforts—
bake sales, car washes, things like that."

(Gee! That sounded familiar!)

That's what I love about my dad. He's the greatest
straight man ever born. I'd been waiting for an open-
ing all evening, and here it was. "Funny you should
say that," I began. They all looked at me, and I told
them about how the Unicorns had discussed all the
same ideas. The sad fact was, no bake sale in the
world was going to raise enough money. But a day's
work in a movie at triple scale would certainly pay
for a new roof and probably leave a little left over for
planting the weedy flower beds in the front of the
building.

Both my parents looked at me as though I was
nuts. "Maria! You're not thinking about going to
Hollywood and looking for work," my mother
gasped. "That's absurd."

"I don't have to," I said. "I don't even have to
leave Sweet Valley." That's when I told them about
Tom Sanders and his offer.

"But Maria," my mother protested. "That's exactly
what we came here to get away from. If you do this
movie, then the next thing we know you'll want to go
audition for a commercial. Then it'll be a TV pilot.

Then, somehow, we'll wind up back in Hollywood and"—she darted a look at my dad, who was glowering thoughtfully—"you'll wind up never getting the education we want you to have to prepare you for real life, in Hollywood or out."

"Now, Frances," my father said, a big smile breaking on his face. (For once, I could tell he was going to be on my side without my having to negotiate with him.) "I think what Maria's doing is a wonderful thing. She's not taking the part for any self-promoting career reason. She's doing it in order to donate the money to a very worthy cause. I think we should applaud her efforts and encourage her."

My mother closed her mouth with a snap just the way she always does when my father sounds incredibly pompous—but is also right, so you can't argue with him. Then she looked at me and we both began to laugh.

I love my dad. I really do. He's terminally stuffy. But I think that's what I like best about him.

"I can't believe it." Mrs. Willard sat at her desk surrounded by papers, wads of used tissue, and piles of estimates from workmen. "I just can't believe it."

It was about the fiftieth time she had said that. She was crying and laughing at the same time, and Mandy and I felt really great.

It was Friday afternoon, and we'd practically run to the Center as soon as the last bell rang so we would have time to tell Mrs. Willard the good news before checking in at the Attic. Mrs. Willard looked at me. "One hears a lot of unflattering things about

Hollywood people. It's nice to meet someone who contradicts all the stereotypes."

"Well, I don't want to suddenly be the ambassador of Hollywood or anything." I laughed. "But I'd settle for being the ambassador of the Unicorns."

Mrs. Willard gave us a grateful look. "You're a wonderful group of girls," she said. "A really special group."

Mandy grabbed my sleeve. "Well, Madame Ambassador and I have got to get going. We're due at the thrift shop at three thirty, and we've got about five minutes before we're late."

We waved good-bye and then practically ran out of the building and down the street toward the main part of town. We turned a corner, then another one, then *flew* through the door of the Attic just on the stroke of three thirty, panting like crazy.

We didn't need to kill ourselves, though. Evie was there, sitting on a stool behind the cash register, doing some scales on the violin. When she saw us, she looked up at the clock, then at our sweating faces, and grinned. "Well, I guess I can report to Grandma that you're reliable. On time—to the second."

We laughed, and Evie got up and came over to me. Much to my surprise, she gave me a hug.

"Hey! What's that for? Punctuality?"

Evie smiled. "Nope. I heard about what you're doing. Raising the money for the day-care center's roof by working in that movie."

"How did you hear?" Mandy asked.

Evi held up that afternoon's edition of the *7 & 8 Gazette*. "It was in the paper today."

I put my hands on my hips as though I was really irritated. "Darn that Elizabeth Wakefield. Sometimes she acts more like a press agent than a reporter."

But I really was pretty tickled. I hadn't looked at the paper yet, even though I had it stuffed in my backpack. The *7 & 8 Gazette* usually gets stacked by the lockers on Friday afternoons, which means it gets printed on Friday mornings. Elizabeth must have stayed up all night last night, writing. That was the only way she could have gotten the story finished and handed in early enough for it to get printed in today's paper.

Evie smiled and put the newspaper down. "Well, anyway," she said with a shy smile, "it just confirms everything I've ever thought about you."

I raised my eyebrows curiously.

"You're brave and spunky and unselfish and really, really talented. Grandma always said you were a good role model for me." She smiled shyly. "She was right."

And with that, she picked up her violin case and hurried out. "'Bye!"

"That was a really nice thing to say," Mandy said softly.

I nodded. I'd had a lot of gushing reviews over the years, but I think I was more flattered by Evie's admiration than by anything else that had ever been said or written about me.

Clara's niece and Evie ran the shop over the weekend. So I spent most of Saturday hanging out with Elizabeth and Jessica. While I was over at the

Wakefields', the guy from the paint store called Jessica and told her the order was ready.

I heard Jessica promise the man she would pick it up that afternoon. But somehow she wound up going to the movies with Ellen. After the movie, they went for ice cream. And then there was nobody at the Wakefields' house to drive her to the store to pick it up. By the time Mr. Wakefield got home, it was too late. The store was closed for the night, and it wasn't open on Sunday.

"I'll do it Monday after school," Jessica said with an unconcerned toss of her head, "when I can get some of the Unicorns to help me carry it. Then I won't need a car."

Elizabeth just shook her head. "Bet you five bucks that paint never gets picked up and those lockers never get repainted," she said to me in a low voice.

"I heard that," Jessica said angrily. "And you'd lose that bet. I'll get it done. Don't worry. It's just that things keep coming up."

"Yeah. Things always 'come up' when you have chores," Elizabeth retorted. "Things like movies, and sales at the mall, and TV quiz shows that you absolutely can't miss, and . . ."

"OK, OK." Jessica grinned good-naturedly. "Next week, I'll get everybody on the job. We'll get the lockers painted in no time."

Elizabeth just gave me a knowing smile. Jessica is loads of fun. But follow-up and follow-through are not her two best sports. In the old days, Elizabeth would have jumped in and taken over the job. But I knew she was trying to change that pattern. And as far as the other

Unicorns were concerned—they were all busy with their own projects. It was up to Jessica to spearhead the painting job. Round 'em up and get 'em moving on it. If she didn't, it wouldn't get done. And if that happened, Mr. Clark was not going to be happy about it.

On Sunday, Mom roped Nina and me into helping her clean out the garage. That took up most of the afternoon, and by the time I finished my homework, had dinner, and took a bath, I realized I hadn't had any time to think about the Unicorns, school, or the movie all day.

But I must have been more tired than I thought, because I was just settling down to have a really good think about everything, when the next thing I knew, the alarm was ringing and it was Monday morning.

The morning went by in a blur and pretty soon it was time for lunch. We were all sitting in the Unicorner when I saw Evie coming out of the lunch line. I knew the Unicorns used to have some rule about getting everybody's permission before asking somebody to sit with us, but I figured the new Unicorns wouldn't care about that stuff. So I raised my arm and waved her over. *"Evie!"* I yelled. "Over here."

Evie's face broke into a big grin. I could tell she was flattered to be asked to sit with a bunch of seventh-graders.

I glanced around the table and noticed two faces looked a little strange—Jessica's and Ellen Riteman's. But everybody else gave Evie a big hello when she sat down.

They all introduced themselves, and then some-body—I think it was Ellen—asked Evie how she knew me.

Evie's fork stopped in midair between her mouth and her plate. "I knew Maria from seeing her on television long before I ever met her in person," Evie explained.

"Huh?" Mary said with a frown.

Evie's eyes got this strange, glowing light in them. "There are some actresses—not many, but my grand-mother's one and Maria's another—who just project right out of the television or the movie screen. They have the kind of screen presence that just gets right into people's hearts and makes them feel that they know that person, not just the character they're play-ing, but the person they are inside."

Elizabeth's eyebrows lifted slightly, and she shot a look at me as if to say, *Is she serious?*

I smothered a giggle. Evie was nearly quoting from an article that had been written about me and Clara around the time the TV movie we made to-gether first aired. The writer of the article had gone way over the top as far as I was concerned, but in her usual enthusiastic way Evie must have taken every word to heart. What could I say? Clearly, Evie had been bitten by the hero-worship bug.

"So Maria was really big stuff," Mary commented with a little twisted smile at the edge of her mouth, as if she didn't know quite how much to believe.

"Oh, yeah!" Evie answered. "She had Hollywood absolutely at her feet. Nobody ever said no to Maria Slater. Not directors. Not agents. Nobody. She was too big a star."

"Evie . . ." I began, hoping to stop the tide. All this gushing praise was getting really embarrassing. I'd forgotten how Evie tended to get carried away, how she could go on and on about stuff. Obviously, she was still a chatterbox. And now that she was over her shyness around everyone, she seemed determined to tell everybody the story of my life.

"She just had that special something that everybody responded to," Evie continued, not even drawing a breath. "Did you know she was once in a commercial for Princess macaroni? And after the first time the commercial went on the air, the company sold, like, *millions* of boxes in one week. It was some kind of advertising record."

I noticed every Unicorn's eyes were turned on me with a mixture of amazement, awe, and surprise. I'd always downplayed my Hollywood successes in Sweet Valley, thinking it would help me fit in better. I mean, I did tell them I was an actress. In fact, I got into terrible trouble when I lied about a movie I was supposedly going to be in. But I never told them the things Evie was telling them now.

"No," Mary said faintly, "I don't think we did know that." She looked around the table at the other Unicorns, as though she was waiting for somebody to speak up and say, *Oh, yeah, I knew all about it.* But nobody did. She exchanged glances with Ellen and Jessica and Mandy and Lila. "Most of us know each other backward and forward," she said with a smile, "but it looks like we still have a lot to learn about our new members."

Lila shifted a little in her seat. "*Do* tell us more,

Maria," she said in a hurt tone of voice, as if she was disappointed in me for not sharing every fact of my life with the other Unicorns.

My stomach sank a little. Evie had gone overboard and now Lila was feeling left out. I didn't need Lila's jealousy. And I didn't need all this reminiscing about bygone glory, either. So I quickly, and determinedly, changed the subject.

"Tell us about your violin lessons," I said to Evie.

Evie's eyes lit up again. "My teacher's name is Mr. Santos and he's fabulous. In fact, I think he's better than Mr. François, who was my teacher in Hollywood."

She looked around the table as if debating whether or not to say anything more. Then she seemed to make up her mind. "I stopped studying with Mr. François because we couldn't afford him anymore," she said, sounding almost defensive. "In fact, we couldn't afford to stay in Beverly Hills anymore. My grandmother just doesn't get as much work as she used to."

Nobody said anything.

"It happens to lots of actresses," Evie said. Her voice was still defensive, but it had a little catch in it, as though she might cry. "It has nothing to do with being talented. My grandmother is a great actress."

There was a short, awkward pause. Then suddenly, Mary jumped in. "*Great* is an understatement. Your grandmother is my very favorite actress of all time."

"Really?" Evie said, her usual chatty demeanor returning.

"Oh, yeah!"

"Mine, too," Mandy added. "And I think it's fabulous that you guys are going to be living here from now on. It's a great place to live. And very economical, according to my mom. My folks are very concerned about cost of living and stuff. My mom's in what she calls a *volatile* industry—which means she could get laid off, maybe."

Elizabeth nodded seriously. "That's what my dad says, too. He's a lawyer, and he says the economy is really cutting into his firm's business."

Jessica dropped her fork in panic. "We're still going to get our allowances, aren't we?"

Everybody began to laugh, and the tense mood of the past few minutes was broken. This wasn't your usual Unicorner conversation.

Let's face it. Most of the Unicorns come from families with plenty of money. Mandy doesn't. And Mary doesn't. They don't have much at all. But Lila's dad is incredibly rich, and everybody else's family is pretty comfortable.

The girls in the Unicorn Club used to be so snobby that everybody always used to try to act rich. And the Unicorns always looked down on girls that didn't come from wealthy families.

Now here they were trying to set Evie at ease about her situation. Make her feel that she wasn't alone. And that it didn't matter.

"What kind of music are you playing?" Elizabeth asked, sounding truly interested. "I really like violin music."

While Evie answered Elizabeth's question, I let my

mind wander a little. I felt proud of the Unicorns. They were acting like true friends. Kind. Considerate. Eager to make an outsider feel welcome. I hadn't made a mistake in joining their club. Not at all. It made me want to get to know them all even better.

A few seconds later, Evie dropped her napkin on her plate and stood, picking up her tray. "Sorry. I've got to leave early to go to the library. I need to listen to a concerto before my lesson this afternoon. And if I don't do it now, I'll never get it done. Thanks for inviting me to sit with you," she said, and smiled.

Everybody smiled and waved, and then nobody said a word as we watched her walk away, drop her tray at the conveyor, and leave the cafeteria.

As soon as she was out the door, Mary leaned forward on her elbows and looked at the group. "OK. What are we going to do to help them? Obviously, they're having major financial problems."

"Bringing more business into the Attic would help," Ellen said.

Mandy snapped her fingers. "I've got it."

"What?" Ellen asked, leaning closer and looking at Mandy.

"We're the Unicorns, right?" Mandy said.

We all nodded, looking a little uncertain.

"That means we're the prettiest, the most popular, and the hippest girls at school. Right?"

"Even if we do say so ourselves," Mary put in.

We all giggled.

"Well, we *are*." Mandy giggled, too, but went on insistently. "So let's put it to good use. Start a thrift-shop dressing trend. Get in on the grunge thing."

"What are you talking about?" Jessica demanded.

"Let's all start wearing thrift-store clothes to school and see if we can make it catch on. See if we can get people to come in and start buying up the clothes."

"That's a great idea," Elizabeth said, and grinned. "But how? You're the only one who knows how to put that stuff together."

"Everybody come by the store this afternoon," Mandy said. "I'll see what I can do about putting together some great looks for everybody."

"All right!" Jessica exclaimed.

She loves anything having to do with clothes and fashion.

"I thought you were going to pick up the paint this afternoon," Elizabeth reminded her.

Jessica's eyes got really big. "Let's get our priorities straight, Elizabeth. We have a chance to help someone here. I think that's more important than lockers, don't you? The paint can wait till tomorrow."

Elizabeth just looked at me and rolled her eyes. "Five bucks," she mouthed in my direction, making me laugh so hard I almost spilled my milk.

Five

I hate to admit this, but by the time I got to English class after lunch, my head was so big I was surprised I could fit it through the door of the classroom. Even though I'd been a little embarrassed by all Evie's praise, I liked hearing it. It had been a long time since anybody had made such a big fuss over me.

I smiled at Rick Hunter, waved at Elizabeth, and then took my usual seat in the front row. I'm good in English and I like the class. The teacher is new. His name is Mr. Hines. He's hard and kind of strict, but he likes my essays and almost always gives me A's.

Within a few minutes, everybody came filing in from the cafeteria and the class was full.

Mr. Hines walked in just as the second bell rang— very tall and straight in his suit and tie. He cleared his throat, put his books on the desk, and then pulled out a file folder full of essays from last week.

"Good afternoon, class," he said formally.

"Good afternoon, Mr. Hines," the class answered. Then we giggled because it all seemed so old-fashioned.

"I've read and marked your essays," he said, beginning to flip through them, "and I'd like to return them to you. There was some very good work in here, and I'm proud of many of you."

I sat back happily in my seat. My self-esteem was way up there already, and an A on an essay would really make me feel great. I knew I would get an A because I had worked really hard on that essay. In fact, I had stayed up practically all night doing it.

Mr. Hines was working his way up the aisle. He handed Rick Hunter his. Rick looked at it and grinned, so I figured he got a good grade. Elizabeth got hers and gave it a brisk little satisfied nod before putting it away, so I knew she had gotten an A.

Then he handed me mine. And when he did, my eyes bugged. Instead of a big proud A at the top, there was a B, and lots of red marks on the page.

I couldn't believe it. Why? I knew I'd worked hard. And right at the top of the page, he'd written "Excellent content." So why did he give me a B?

I made up my mind to talk to him about it after class. And as soon as the bell rang, I hurried up to his desk. "Mr. Hines?" I said, pitching my voice a little higher so that it sounded pleasant. (It's a little acting tip I learned years ago.)

Mr. Hines looked up from his desk. "Yes, Maria?"

I held out my paper. "I don't understand why I got a B on this paper. I worked very hard and was sure that I would get an A."

Mr. Hines frowned and pointed toward the paper with his pen. "There is nothing wrong with your content, Maria. But as you can see here . . . here . . . and here"—he tapped the paper with his pen—"you have made grammatical and spelling errors that brought your grade down."

I could feel my face fall a little. I couldn't believe he was really going to lower my grade a whole letter just because of a few spelling mistakes. Nobody should be that unreasonable, I thought. All he needed was a little coaxing and he'd raise the grade to an A.

I straightened my shoulders and smiled so wide that both rows of teeth showed. It was what my agent used to call "the most winning smile in America." Part apology, part entreaty, part affection. "Don't you think you could overlook the spelling mistakes this one time," I asked sweetly, "if I rewrite the paper, correct the mistakes, and write a little extra essay on punctuation?"

I raised my eyebrows just a tad and dropped my chin. "Please," I added in a little whispery voice.

It was perfect. I half expected to hear a studio audience go, "Aawwwww" and a director yell, *"Cut! Print!"* It was classic Maria Slater stuff.

I stared at Mr. Hines, waiting for him to cave in. But he didn't blink. He didn't smile. And he showed no signs whatsoever of saying, "Aawwwww."

"Maria," he said in a flat voice. "I am not in the habit of changing grades for students. You earned a B on this essay, and the grade will stand. I applaud your desire for better grades. But if you want them, you're going to have to earn them. That means you're going to have to work harder and do the work right the first time. Please don't ask me for special favors. It's not fair to me, and you do yourself a disservice. Do I make myself clear?"

My cheeks felt as though they were on fire. "Yes, sir," I mumbled, stuffing the paper into my backpack. I hurried out of the classroom feeling completely deflated. I'd never been so humiliated in my life. I'd really bombed in there. The only good thing about it was that nobody else had been around to see it.

I was embarrassed. But most of all, I was worried. Really worried.

My famous smile had left Mr. Hines completely unmoved. In the old days, that smile had gotten me anything I wanted. Directors, agents, managers, assistants, cameramen, wardrobe people, hairdressers, and waiters would fall all over themselves to do something for me if I smiled at them like that.

That smile was on the cover of *Folks* magazine, for gosh sakes. Now that smile couldn't even get an English teacher to let me do some extra credit for a better grade.

Was I losing my touch? Losing my talent? Losing my ability to make people feel something?

Then I saw Evie wave at me from the other end of the hall. The smile on her face was so warm, so friendly, that I couldn't help but feel better. It was nice to know somebody still thought I had star quality.

What happened in there was a fluke, I told myself. Just a fluke. For some reason, Mr. Hines was not impressed by my acting talent. But I still had it. I knew I did. I could see it in Evie's eyes.

*   *   *

Jessica and Lila got to the Attic first and started flipping through the racks. Over the next twenty minutes, everybody else arrived.

Jessica pulled an old rayon forties-style house-dress with a fluted hem from the rack. "Wow! This is really cool. Think it'll fit me?"

"Go in the dressing room and try it on," Mandy instructed. "In fact, everybody look around. See if you can find one piece you like. Then we'll build outfits around them." She handed Elizabeth a pad and a pencil. "Elizabeth will be our accountant, so be sure to keep track of the prices. Some of the tags are kind of loose. And be sure she knows what you're getting."

Everybody nodded and started eagerly looking at everything, *ooh*ing and *ahh*ing at all the neat stuff. Ellen Riteman immediately found a pair of incredibly ugly platforms that somehow looked incredibly wonderful on her. I could tell she was going to have those shoes on for the next three months.

Since I had my funky outfit already (the one from the first day), I decided to see if I could make myself useful around the rest of the store. So I started straightening knickknacks on the shelf.

The bell on the door tinkled and in walked a young couple, who headed directly for the furniture section of the shop. They looked incredibly affluent with their perfect tans and haircuts and their name-brand casual clothes.

I decided to wait on them. "May I help you?" I asked, hurrying over to join them.

The husband motioned toward one of the wing

chairs with his expensive sunglasses. "We just moved into a home and we need some furniture." He grinned at his wife. "We just got married and we don't have anything yet. Our place looks like a haunted house."

Ah-hah! *Bingo!* I was really excited. This was going to be an easy sale. They needed furniture. We had furniture for sale. Clara would be thrilled to make some money. And to top it off, the salesperson in charge was *the* Maria Slater—the girl with the face that had sold truckloads of Princess macaroni and Softee toilet tissue.

"Well," I said, breaking into a broad smile, "you've come to the right place. This wing chair here is a classic—as well as a good buy."

The wife nodded and straightened her headband, but she didn't look too enthusiastic. In fact, she kind of sneered. Maybe they thought it wasn't cool to get excited over secondhand furniture.

"No holes anywhere in the upholstery," I pointed out. "The springs are in good condition, and . . ."

I noticed that her attention seemed to be wandering. Her eyes were roaming toward the window, and she looked at something on the street outside.

This section of town is a popular shopping district, and both sides of the street are dotted with shops and boutiques and galleries. There are also two ice-cream parlors, a bookstore, and a pharmacy where kids from Sweet Valley Middle School sometimes like to hang out instead of at the mall. People were streaming up and down the sidewalks, and I saw a lot of kids I knew from school go by.

I began moving my hands around. That's an old

theater trick. When you think you're losing the attention of the audience, animate your lines a little and get it focused back on you. "The color's neutral but not boring—it will go with anything else you decide to buy later," I said, pitching my voice higher and giving it some life.

The husband nodded absently, but he was now looking out the window, too. "There's an art gallery across the street," he said in a really affected voice. He turned to his wife. "You know, maybe it's better to start out with one or two really *important* pieces of art. I think I'd rather sit on folding chairs than waste money on secondhand junk."

Junk!

It was all I could do not to inform Mr. Snobhead that this "junk" happened to be some of the most elegant furniture in the world. Clara's house had been beautiful, and I knew the furniture was top quality. But I was trying to sell, not educate. So I kept hammering away.

"It's only ten dollars!" I said breathlessly. *"Ten dollars!"* I repeated a little louder—the way they teach you to do in commercials.

But by now, neither one of them was even listening. "Honey, look out there. There's a bunch of kids around our new Jeep," the husband said.

I stepped between them, in front of the window. *"You'll never find a better buy!"* I practically yelled. And I was smiling so hard it was making my ears hurt.

But the wife sort of craned her neck so she could look past me, over my shoulder. "They'll get fingerprints all over it," she said with a concerned frown.

I glanced out the window and saw some of the guys from school standing around a big, shiny, brand-new black Jeep. The kind that is really popular with young, rich types. It was the kind of vehicle that really screams for attention. So why were they getting so bent out of shape that it was attracting some attention? Sheesh!

Still, they were a challenge. A test of my charisma, talent, and salesmanship.

"Hey!" I said, determined to make one last effort to make the sale, even if I had to cash in on my past glory. "Do I look familiar to you?"

The husband frowned. "You're not the girl who's always riding her bike through our flower bed, are you?"

"No," I answered in an offended tone. I was in the seventh grade, for heaven's sake. An actress. A professional. An honor-roll student. And here they were acting like I was Dennis the Menace.

The husband looked at me suspiciously. "You look a lot like that girl. We don't like kids riding bikes through our flower beds."

Kids! "Hey!" I protested. "I don't even have a bike. And for your information, I'm not a kid—"

"John," the lady said, grabbing her husband's sleeve and cutting me off. "Look out there. Those boys are touching our Jeep," she said in this panicky voice. "I knew we should have parked in the lot."

"Kids!" the husband sighed. "Come on, honey. We'd better get out there right now before they ruin our wax job completely. We'll put the Jeep in the lot, then we'll hit the art gallery."

"Hey!" I yelled as they hurried toward the door. "Don't you want the wing chair?"

They didn't answer.

"It's only ten dollars!" I shouted.

They were pushing the door open.

"It's a major bargain!"

But the next thing I knew, they were outside, shooing away Rick Hunter, Randy Mason, and a few of the other guys from school.

"Rats," I muttered under my breath.

I watched them climb into their fancy Jeep and drive away.

Then I sat down in the wing chair and stared glumly at an oil painting of the south of France that had hung in Clara's front hall in her house in Hollywood.

What was the matter with me? Had I just lost everything? My charisma. My winning smile. My charm. My sales ability.

A few years ago I was a major Hollywood actress. Now I couldn't even sell a ten-dollar wing chair with tap dancing and cartwheels.

As I watched the guys horsing around on the other side of the street, shoving each other and laughing, I felt a cold, choking fear in my throat.

Maybe whatever had made me *the* Maria Slater was gone. Maybe I'd outgrown it. Or the public had outgrown me. I wasn't a movie star masquerading as a regular person anymore. I really was a regular person. No different from anybody else. No more talented than anybody else.

I felt a tear trickling down my cheek and heard Shawn Brockaway's voice ringing in my ear: "You're just a washed-up has-been." That's what she had said to me when she'd come to Sweet Valley to film last year. I'd laughed then, because the words hadn't meant anything. They were just insults from somebody who didn't know anything about me.

Now those words had come back to haunt me. Because I was afraid they might be true.

"What's the matter, Maria?" Mandy asked, appearing beside me. "You can't expect to sell everything in the store in just a few days."

I smiled and swallowed the lump in my throat. Mandy was right. I was totally overreacting.

So Mr. Hines wouldn't change my essay grade. Big deal. He probably hated kids—just like that awful couple that had just come in here. Why was I letting people like that shake my confidence?

Over the next hour, there were a few customers in the store. I sold a couple of prints. A coffee table. A few wineglasses. But most of the action was in the back with the Unicorns.

The girls looked wild. Absolutely wild. All the girls have good fashion sense—but Mandy had really turned them into some show-stoppers. You never saw such outrageous, high-fashion getups, and all out of stuff people had given away. Just goes to show you—one woman's junk is another woman's couture.

The bell rang again and I hurried over to greet the young man who had walked in. He had a very tentative look on his face and a big manila envelope under his arm. He looked at me, then grinned. "Maria Slater?" he said.

"That's me," I answered.

He shook my hand. "I'm Phil Silkin, Tom's assistant. He asked me to bring you a copy of the script."

He removed the thick script from the envelope and showed me where paper clips were attached to the few pages that contained my part.

By now, the rest of the Unicorns were beginning to gather around and were eagerly reading over my shoulder.

"Oh, my God!" Mary shrieked. "It's a love scene."

Phil grinned. "Well, sort of. It's a comic romantic scene."

"It's got a kiss in it," Jessica breathed enviously.

My heart dropped to my stomach with a sickening thud. A love scene? I'd never done a love scene before. Comic or not. I'd never been old enough before. Suddenly, my palms were wet with sweat. I had no idea how to do a scene like this. What was I going to do?"

"Who's the lucky guy that Maria gets to kiss?" Ellen asked, giggling.

"Maria will be playing opposite Brad Marshall," Phil answered.

There was a long, stunned, hushed pause.

Then the entire group let out an earsplitting squeal. (A squeal in which I, by the way, did not participate.)

Brad Marshall is one of the hottest teen stars in the business. I'd met him a few times over the years. I'd even worked with him once or twice.

But what nobody knew—or had ever known— was that I was absolutely head over heels in crush with him. I mean, the guy is major adorable. Skin the color of caramel. Long, dark lashes. Tall. Athletic. And really sweet.

And he wasn't just a hunk, either. He was a really talented, sensitive actor. Somebody who always got his scenes right. Always found just the right expression, inflection, and body posture to convey whatever it was he was trying to convey.

In other words, the last person in the world I'd want to play opposite in my first love scene. What if I'm an awful kisser? Or what if I really blow the scene? He'll think I'm a total geeky, nerdy adolescent no-talent.

Uggghhhhhhh!

Just as I was considering dropping out of the whole project, Jessica sighed enviously. "I wish I could earn a new roof for the day-care center by kissing Brad Marshall."

The day-care center.

Double *uggghhhhhhh!* In all the confusion, I'd forgotten why I was doing this in the first place. I couldn't drop out. Not now. Not when all those kids were counting on me.

Six

I didn't sleep well that night, so the next morning I decided I had to force myself to put it all—the movie, Brad Marshall, everything—out of my mind for at least the next couple of days. I had a math test coming up and another English essay due soon.

The shoot wasn't until Monday, and I knew if I started thinking about it too soon, not only would I blow my schoolwork, I'd freeze up and blow the scene, too.

The night before I had read the script all the way through. It really was fun. And if I hadn't been so terrified about my scene, I really would have been looking forward to it.

You weren't going to think about it, I reminded myself fiercely as I approached school.

Just before I walked through the front doors, I adjusted the beaded tunic I was wearing over my T-shirt and bicycle shorts, and pulled my floppy crushed-velvet hat down over my eyes. It was the thrift-store out-fit Mandy had put together. I hoped the rest of the Unicorns had kept their promise to wear thrift-store funk to school today. If not, I would be the only one. And I sure would look stupid.

But the second I got inside, I quit worrying.

The first person I spotted was Mary. Mandy had helped her get all done up like a riding instructor from the twenties. She had on riding boots and a red hunting coat, and her short hair was styled with a spit curl over her forehead. Then she'd taken a black bowler hat and covered it with conservation buttons.

The outfit looked great, and it really showed off Mary's tall, slim figure.

Lots of people had gathered around her and the rest of the Unicorns.

"You guys look great," Rick Hunter said, looking at Jessica's forties-style dress with real admiration. "What's this all about? Is it costume week for the Unicorns or what?"

"It's funk week for everybody," Mandy answered. "Believe it or not, not one of these outfits cost over fif-teen dollars."

"You're kidding," Caroline Pearce exclaimed, fin-gering the cashmere of Elizabeth's pink sweater set, which she wore with a poodle skirt and pearls. "I'd love to have something that looks like this. And my clothing budget is never big enough."

"Well, it's got to be bigger than Randy Mason's," Peter DeHaven joked, pointing to Randy's short-sleeved shirt. There was an ink stain on the pocket. "He's been wearing that same shirt for three days."

"I have not," Randy protested. "I've been wearing the same *pen*. It leaks."

Everybody roared with laughter. Randy Mason was the president of the class last year. He's sort of a nerd. But he's the kind of nerd that everybody likes and is really popular in his own weird way. He's also some kind of genius. He's always walking around with a pocket full of pens, and sometimes they leak through his shirt pocket.

"Tell you what," Rick said to the crowd that had gathered around, asking the Unicorns questions about this garment and that. He reached into his pocket and pulled out five dollars. "I'll contribute five dollars toward getting Randy a Mandy Miller makeover."

"I'll put in four," Peter DeHaven immediately volunteered.

Everybody was laughing, including Randy, as people pitched in a dollar . . . fifty cents . . . assorted change, bringing the fund up to fifteen dollars.

"But I don't want to be made over," Randy protested weakly through his laughter.

Rick and Peter, his two best friends, put their arms around him. "There's nothing to be afraid of, buddy," Rick said seriously. "Peter and I will be there the whole time."

"Right," Peter confirmed. "If they try to give you a mohawk or something like that, you can count on us to put a stop to it."

The whole thing was turning into a great joke—and a pretty good way of drawing people into the shop. Everybody was saying they wanted to come by, look around, and see Randy get a makeover.

The Unicorns all exchanged meaningful looks. Our plan was working. The shop was going to be packed this afternoon.

By four thirty, I was dragging two more cartons from the back of the storeroom. They were heavy, but my heart felt light as air. The Attic was packed, and some of the kids were turning into serious shoppers. The Randy Mason makeover was going on in the back, and tons of kids had come to watch and have a good laugh.

Randy had been a great sport, too. He let Mandy try all sorts of weird things on him.

"Fabulous!" Mandy exclaimed finally, putting the finishing touches on his outfit.

I hurried over to join the others, and everybody who'd been watching now burst into appreciative applause.

"I don't know," Randy murmured. He looked skeptical and a little afraid—as if maybe we were making fun of him.

But we weren't. We really weren't. Mandy had worked her magic, and Randy Mason had been transformed from a seminerdy seventh-grade science fan into a totally hip-looking New Age geekoid. He looked like a cross between Buddy Holly and James Dean, with just a touch of Elvis. He had on thick black-framed glasses, a cardigan, a short-sleeved white shirt, and a narrow tie. Black ribbed dress socks and high-topped red basketball shoes. No belt on the jeans, so they hung low on his hips.

"You really think I should wear this to school?" he

asked in a nervous voice, looking at Rick.

"Man, Randy"—Rick laughed—"if I didn't know you were Randy Mason, I'd think you were somebody famous who had just come to town. You look like a rock star or something."

It had been a ball—so much fun I had forgotten my own troubles. Randy Mason had never been my idea of Cinderella, but we had definitely transformed him into the Prince of Trendy.

As usual, Elizabeth was acting as accountant. "Let's see, there's the sweater and the other pullover," she muttered as she wrote down all the inventory numbers and the prices, "but the rest of it . . . let's see . . ." she murmured. "That's twenty-five cents for the tie . . . a dollar for the shirt . . ."

Pretty soon, she handed Randy a neatly handprinted bill. He gave the bill to Rick, who was in charge of the makeover fund. "Geez, and change back from your dollar," Rick said as he gave Elizabeth some bills and she handed him back a couple of coins.

"Who's next?" Mandy cried.

"*Me!*" Rick, Peter, Caroline Pearce, and about twenty other people all shouted at once.

"One at a time," Mandy insisted, laughing. "Rick, let's see what we can do with you."

"OK, but I'm definitely next," Caroline said, grinning.

"Then me," Peter insisted.

Just then, another huge group of kids came in the front door, laughing and looking around. Evie was with them, and she came immediately over to me.

"Wow!" she said. "What's going on here? I've never seen so many people in the store."

"We figured if we started a thrift-store shopping trend, it would really help you and your grandmother make some money," said a familiar voice behind me.

I whirled around angrily, saw Jessica, and stomped down hard on her toe. Honestly! Jessica can be so tactless. What a dumb thing to say.

I was sure Evie would square her shoulders and announce coldly that she and her grandmother didn't need help from us. But instead she looked really touched. "I can't believe it," she whispered. "You did this for me? For us?"

Jessica poked out her tongue at me as if to say, *See? You worry too much,* and then she grinned. "We really like you. And we like to help the people we like."

Evie threw her arms around my neck. "I think the Unicorns are the greatest club in the world," she said, her voice a little choked. "And I think you're the greatest person I've ever known."

Just then, Elizabeth appeared and tapped Jessica. "I thought you said you were going to see about the paint today. Mom said the man at the store called again and—"

"Elizabeth," Jessica warned, putting her hand up as if to say, *Chill.* "Not now," she whispered loudly. She gestured toward me, with Evie's arms wrapped around my neck. Then she shook her head as if Elizabeth were being incredibly insensitive. "You really know how to wreck a party," she said in a superior tone of voice. "I don't think now is the time to talk about paint." Then, totally uninvited, Jessica threw her arms around me and Evie, joining in our hug and giving us a big squeeze.

That Jessica! Whatever's going on, she's just got to be in the middle of it. I mean, what a ham!

Elizabeth groaned and I just cracked up.

Seven

"So you're really going to do a love scene with Brad Marshall?" Nina asked breathlessly. "Aren't you thrilled to death?"

It was Tuesday night. We both had our night-gowns on and we were sitting on my bed talking.

"Actually, it kind of makes me feel like throwing up."

"Probably because you've always had such a big crush on him," Nina said casually, picking up a nail file and going to work on one of her nails.

"What do you mean, I've always had a crush on him?" I shot back, snatching the nail file from Nina.

"Haven't you?"

"No." My face flushed at the lie. "How can you say something so . . . so . . . so . . ."

"True?" Nina giggled, cocking her head to the side and giving me this knowing look. "Come on, Maria. When you two were shooting that cereal commercial, even I could see you were crazy about Brad. And when you guested on his sitcom a few years ago, you followed him around like a lost puppy."

"That's not true!" I yelled. I picked up a pillow and hit Nina over the head.

"It is too," she said with a laugh from beneath the pillow. Then she popped her head out. "But what are you getting so worked up about? Everybody thought it was cute."

"I was a little kid then. I was playing his little sister or something. It's different now."

Nina put her lips together and made obnoxious smacking noises. "It's different now," she said in a sappy voice that was supposed to be mine. She batted her eyelashes and laced her fingers under her chin. "I'm all grown up now, Brad. Old enough to kiss you." Then she made one long-drawn-out squeaking kiss noise.

I stifled a laugh—this *was* kind of funny—then lifted my chin firmly. "Clearly, it's very difficult for amateurs to appreciate the difficulty of convincingly conveying affection for another individual in front of four cameras, a crew, and a director," I joked in a fake, superior voice.

Nina picked up the pillow and walloped me with it. "Oh, don't go getting your feelings hurt. I'm just kidding you because I'm jealous. I'd love to kiss Brad Marshall—in front of anybody."

"You wouldn't if you knew how hard acting really was," I said, suddenly glum again. Nina didn't know it, but she was hitting all my panic buttons. What if I accidentally *did* make squeaking smacking noises during the kiss in our scene? What if my stomach growled? What if the fact that I had a crush on him made me absolutely unable to remember a single line when he was standing close to me?

"What's the matter?" Nina said softly. "I'm sorry I teased you. There's something really bothering you, isn't there?"

"I'm worried that I'm not really a good enough actress to hold my own in a scene with him," I confided. I told her about not being able to get Mr. Hines to change my grade. Then I told her about not being able to sell that couple a chair. She thought both those stories were funny. But then I told her about seeing myself in an old made-for-TV movie I'd watched on a local cable station just before dinner.

I'd always remembered myself as being pretty good in that part. In fact, I had scenes from it on my demo reel. But this evening when I'd watched it, I hadn't thought I was very good at all. "Nina," I said, trying to explain, "I didn't see an actress on the screen. I saw this precocious little kid with a case of the cutes and a bag full of tired old acting tricks. That's not going to fly in this movie."

Nina flopped back on the pillows and folded her arms behind her head, staring at the ceiling for a long time. Finally, she said, "I pulled out an old essay of mine last week. One I wrote a couple of years ago. I'd always thought it was the best thing I'd ever written. But when I read it again, I thought it sounded like garbage." She sat up and threw out her hands. "But I don't think that means I'm a bad writer, Maria. I think it means I've gotten better. I've gotten older, my tastes have matured, and my style has gotten more sophisticated."

"So you're saying you think I can do it?"

"I'm saying acting is a talent you've got. It doesn't go away. You may not have done it for a couple of years. But believe me, when you get up there in front of the camera and the lights, you'll be better than ever."

She stood up and stretched. "Well, that's all the pep talk you get from me tonight, Ms. Slater. I'm going to bed." She grinned. "By the way, I hear the Attic was jammed today. Are you guys staging some kind of publicity stunt?"

"We're starting a trend," I explained. "And so far, we've made a pile of money for Clara and Evie."

Nina smiled. "That's nice. Really nice. When you joined the Unicorns, I thought you were nuts. But now I see it was a good thing."

She came over and yanked my ponytail. "Good night, Unicorn."

"Good night," I said as she left the room and closed the door softly behind her.

I still wasn't sleepy, but I'd finished my homework and I didn't feel like listening to music.

The script was sitting on my desk. I couldn't help thinking about what Nina had just said. Was she right? Would I still be good? Could I even be better?

Even though I'd promised myself I wouldn't, I decided to run through a few of my lines in front of the mirror. I got out of bed, opened the script, and walked over to the mirror to try a line of my dialogue.

"What do you *steal*?" I asked curiously, reading

the highlighted line off the page.

No. That delivery was all wrong. I sounded too childish.

I shook my head to loosen the muscles in my neck and tried again.

"*What* do you steal?" I asked again. This time, I put a little flirtatious note in my voice and batted my eyelashes.

Gag! I looked like Ellen Riteman doing an imitation of Jessica when she's flirting with Rick Hunter.

"What do *you* steal?" I whispered, pretending to be frightened.

Worse!

I slammed the script shut and threw it on the floor. What did Nina know? I wasn't any better. I was horrible. Just horrible.

Not only that—I was *ugly.*

I stared at myself in the mirror. When had my nose gotten so big? It was practically the size of a potato. And was that a pimple forming on my chin? The shoot was on Monday. By then, it would be big enough to paint a smiley face on.

And my hair!

Forget it. Some people have bad hair days. I was having a bad hair *life.*

And there was no sense thinking it wasn't going to show. One thing about the camera: it doesn't lie.

Eight

After my little panic attack the night before, I tried to make sure I started the day on Wednesday as calmly as possible. I did deep-breathing exercises every time I felt myself starting to lose it. And I just threw myself into my schoolwork. You would have thought I was bucking for valedictorian or something.

The other big thing that kept me going was the thrift shop. The kids at school were getting totally carried away with the look, and I couldn't help feeling a little twinge of pride that the Unicorns had managed to start a major trend in such a short amount of time. Basically we're talking a day.

Even some of the teachers came into the store late yesterday afternoon and bought some funky vintage stuff. Mr. Hines bought a tie from the fifties. The Unicorns' thrift-store trend was turning out to be a big hit.

As long as I concentrated on the good things that

were going on, I was able to keep from panicking. What can I say? I was making a motto out of "Acc*en*tuate the positive. E*lim*inate the negative."

I was succeeding pretty well until just after third period, when Janet Nash hissed at me from behind the door of the girls' room. "Maria," she whispered, beckoning me to join her.

Janet is in the drama club with me. She's a good actress, especially at character stuff. She's almost always a second lead, and I guess you could sort of say she's my best friend in the drama club—except for Mandy, of course. Anyway, Janet and I try to help each other out whenever we can.

"What's up?" I asked quickly. I could tell something was wrong from the look on her face.

"I was just over in the main prop room," she said. "You know, the one next to the teachers' meeting room." Her shoulders were slumped and she looked really miserable. "I wasn't trying to eavesdrop," she blurted, "but I couldn't help but overhear."

I put my hand on her shoulder. "Hey. Calm down. Sometimes you can't help overhearing conversations. Try not to get so upset."

"But what I heard was about you," she said, looking around to be sure no one could hear.

"What about me?" I asked, my heart beginning to pound.

"Maria," she whispered, "you didn't get the lead in the play."

I was so stunned, I couldn't even answer. My mouth fell open, but I couldn't think of anything to say.

"They're giving it to Marion Weinstein," she added unhappily.

I still couldn't think of anything to say. Marion Weinstein is good. But I'm better. At least I'd thought I was better. Apparently nobody else did, though—at least, not anymore.

"I thought you'd want to know," Janet said. "I know you were counting on it, and sometimes finding out something like that along with everybody else . . ." Her voice trailed off. She didn't have to finish. I knew what she meant. And she was right. If I'd gone up to the bulletin board where the roles are usually posted and found this out with everybody standing around me, craning their necks to see who got what role, I might have burst into tears in front of everybody. At least this way, I could do my crying in advance, and then be gracious about it when the announcement was made.

"Thanks for telling me," I said.

"You won't tell anybody I told?" she asked fearfully. "I mean, the roles won't be posted until next week, and nobody's supposed to know anything."

"Don't worry!" I assured her.

Did she really think I was going to blab it all over school? It was bad enough that I was a washed-up no-talent. There was no need to announce it all over the place. It wasn't exactly the kind of thing I wanted everybody to know.

Then I remembered the movie! I knew I couldn't get out of it. I had to do it in order to get the money for the roof for the day-care center. But I also knew that a lot of film wound up on the cutting-room floor.

The scene I was in wasn't absolutely essential to the movie. It was one of a series of scenes. If I was really awful, all that would happen was they would cut the scene out of the movie.

So what if I made a fool of myself by being awful in the role? Brad Marshall would think I was a geek. And Tom Sanders would go back to Hollywood and say I was a no-talent. But they'd have to pay me for the work I'd done. Then they could cut the scene, and none of my friends at school would ever have to know what happened. I could just say they cut it for length or something.

The muscles in my shoulders began to relax. Things weren't as bad as they seemed. Things were never as bad as they seemed. Why did I always seem to forget that? There was always a way out.

Just then, somebody tapped me on the shoulder. I whirled around and saw Peter DeHaven wearing a student messenger ribbon. (It's a big honor. Some kids get to be student messengers for the principal's office, and instead of reporting to study halls during their free periods, they get to deliver things and go look for people and stuff like that.)

"Maria," Peter said. "Mr. Clark wants you to come to his office."

"Normally, I would never agree to such a disruption of our class schedule," Mr. Clark was saying in his deep, authoritarian voice, "but I think in this case, it would be uncharitable to withhold my permission."

"All right!" Tom Sanders said in happy voice.

When I got to Mr. Clark's office, Tom Sanders was there with a thirty-five millimeter camera. He'd told Mr. Clark all about my being in the movie and how I was going to donate the money I earned to the day-care center.

What he wanted was to follow me around school and take some pictures of me sitting in class, talking with other students, and doing all kinds of typical school things.

He said it would be good publicity for the movie. He said that probably lots of magazines would want to write articles on me—"Child Star Stages Comeback in Tom Sanders's Latest Movie," that sort of thing.

I wished I felt as enthusiastic as he looked, standing there in his leather jacket, jeans, and ponytail. Like a giant-sized middle schooler. It was really kind of funny seeing him sitting in Mr. Clark's office. He looked so hip and Mr. Clark looked so square.

For a funny moment, I felt as if Tom Sanders were in Mr. Clark's office because he was in trouble.

But the next thing I knew, Mr. Clark was graciously showing us both out of his office and shaking Tom's hand. "It was a pleasure to meet you, Mr. Sanders. Let me know if I can assist you in any way at all."

"Thanks a lot," Tom answered with a warm smile. Then he gave a friendly nod to the secretary and a couple of kids who were waiting in the outer office—probably because they really were in trouble.

Tom put his arm over my shoulder. "Let's go take some pictures," he said. "Where's a good place to start?"

Tom Sanders was a nice man, I decided. A really,

really nice man. I felt bad that I was going to take his money when I wasn't qualified to do the work he was hiring me to do. It wasn't fair. I knew the budget on his film was tight. There probably wasn't any extra money for another actress if they had to reshoot the scene.

Day-care center or no day-care center. Roof or no roof. I just couldn't go through with it. I could never quit, but maybe I could get him to fire me.

"You know, Tom," I began, making my voice sound deep and mature, "I've been giving this a lot of thought. Are you sure audiences will accept me in a teen role? After all, they've always known me as a child. It's very hard to sell child stars as adults."

"Are you kidding? I think it'll go over great. Probably pull them into the theaters. Everybody will want to see what you look like and how you've grown up."

"But the scene is tricky. Comedy is a hard thing to pull off," I said, trying another tack. "You've got a tight budget. Wouldn't it be better to play it safe and use a more seasoned actress?"

He grinned. "I didn't get this far by playing it safe."

Darn. Clearly, he wasn't going to take the bait.

"You know, I think I may be taller than Brad Marshall," I said, making one last desperate attempt. "And there's a kiss at the end of the scene."

Tom grinned and shrugged again. "So he can stand on a box. He won't be the first." He grabbed my hand and tugged. "Now, come on. What's our first stop? Algebra class?"

"You wouldn't like it," I said. "Very little atmosphere and . . ."

"Maria," he said, "do I get the impression you're trying to back out of our deal? I know we didn't sign a contract. But we shook hands. You can ask anybody in the business and they'll tell you my word is as good as my signature. I'd be very disappointed to find out yours isn't."

"Of course not," I sputtered, even though he'd hit the nail right on the head. "Don't be ridiculous. I just wanted to be sure you didn't have any second thoughts."

"None at all," he said, then grinned. "Now, let's go."

"This is great!" Tom shouted gleefully, snapping away with his camera as I opened my locker along with about twenty other kids, most of whom were decked out in thrift-store duds.

"This is the funkiest group of middle-schoolers I've ever seen."

Mandy, who was standing next to me, winked.

"Come on, come on," Tom said, his enthusiasm beginning to affect everybody. "Gather in and let me get some shots of the rest of you."

"Unicorns first!" Jessica shouted.

Ellen, Elizabeth, Lila, Mandy, Evie, Jessica, and Mary all gathered around me and struck goofy poses.

"Great!" Tom shouted. "Fabulous. Wonderful. Awesome," he said as we rearranged ourselves over and over, striking pose after pose—some silly, some high-fashion, and some sexy.

Tom lowered the camera and deftly changed the

film while we all giggled. Then he looked up and saw Randy Mason, Rick Hunter, and Peter DeHaven coming down the hall with a bunch of other guys that Mandy had dressed.

"Hey, guys! Can I get some shots of you with the girls?" he asked.

"Sure," Peter agreed with a grin, hurrying toward us.

Tom looked at the group of students gathering around us in the hall and began pointing to people. "That's a great outfit. Let me get you . . . and you . . . and you . . ."

It was great. For the next fifteen minutes, Tom shot about three rolls of film of all the kids at school. And the kids loved it. It all seemed so glamorous.

"Hey!" Tom said, snapping his fingers. "I've got a great idea." He turned to me. "Maria. Let's shoot your scene right here at school instead of in a studio."

"What!" I croaked, my throat closing up. I had a horrible feeling I knew what he was getting at.

Tom pointed all around him. "If Mr. Clark agrees, we'll shoot the scene right here in this hall. Against that bank of lockers." He pointed to the lockers that still had the purple stripe.

"And," he added, grinning broadly at the whole group of students, "we'll use the students of Sweet Valley Middle School as extras."

"*All right!*" the crowd screamed.

"We're going to be in the movies!" Jessica shouted gleefully.

Tom held up his hands, and immediately the crowd became quiet. "The name of the movie is *Secondhand Rose,* and I want the whole film to have a funky, thrift-shop look. So if you don't have some-thing to wear that looks like that, go to the Attic and see Mandy." He pointed to Mandy, who blushed with pleasure. "She'll help you put something together."

The crowd erupted again in excited chatter, then suddenly became quiet as Mr. Clark materialized.

"Mr. Clark," Tom began in an eager voice.

"I heard," Mr. Clark said.

Say no, I pleaded mentally. *Say no. PLEASE say no.* I didn't want to shoot my scene at school. I didn't want all these people standing around watching me be awful. I didn't want to see them start to shift and whisper when Tom yelled, *"Take twenty-five"* in that impatient voice that directors use when they're at their wits' end from working with no-talents.

"It's fine with me if you want to shoot a scene here at school and use some of our students," Mr. Clark said.

My stomach sank down into my shoes.

"But . . ." He looked at Jessica. "I do not want to leave America with the impression that our school is peopled by juvenile delinquents with no respect for their school. So"—he glared at her—"I expect that bank of lockers to be repainted by the day of the shoot. Do I make myself clear?"

"Yes, Mr. Clark," Jessica said meekly.

Before anybody could say anything else, there was a surprised murmur from the back of the crowd. Then the crowd sort of parted with this awed sigh.

Then my heart just went *boom*.

Coming through the crowd, walking right toward me, was Brad Marshall. And he was even more handsome than I remembered. My knees buckled.

"Ah, Brad!" Tom said. He turned to me. "I asked him to come by if he had time so we could shoot a couple of pictures of you two together."

But I could barely hear Tom's voice through the buzz that was surrounding my brain.

Brad Marshall, Brad Marshall, Brad Marshall, my heart was thumping.

He was standing next to me now. "Hi," he said. "I'm really glad to see you again, Maria. It's been a long time." *Too long,* I thought fuzzily. He bent down and kissed me lightly on the cheek.

Did you catch that? He bent *down.* That meant he wasn't shorter than I was. He was taller.

I felt an elbow nudge me. "Maria," Mandy whispered. "He's talking to you."

I forced the corners of my mouth to turn up and hoped it looked like a smile. "It's great to see you again, too," I said.

Why did my voice sound so high and squeaky?

"Stand closer," Tom instructed.

Brad moved closer to me and I moved in closer under his arm.

"Now, smile."

Easy for him to say. He wasn't slated to make a total fool of himself on Monday in front of Brad Marshall, the Unicorn Club, and every other kid at Sweet Valley Middle School.

Nine

I didn't sleep that night. Not one wink. I don't mean I *felt* as if I were awake all night. I really *was* awake all night. I just couldn't stop thinking about how terrible it was going to be.

Even though I'd given up my career a couple of years ago, there were still people who respected me because I'd been a professional actress. Supposedly, a good one.

I didn't want to lose my reputation. I didn't want to lose the respect of the people I'd worked with in the business. It was better to quit while you were ahead, I finally decided around four o'clock in the morning. But how? I couldn't quit.

The Center needed a new roof.

I turned over with a big sigh and whacked my pillow with my fist. I felt trapped. And feeling trapped just made me feel more angry. Why couldn't I quit if I wanted to? Why was it my responsibility to buy the

Center a new roof? I'd given money to charity when I was working. Lots of money. I'd appeared at lots of benefits, too. I'd done my bit. There was no reason to feel guilty about some little day-care center.

But what was I going to do about my handshake deal with Tom Sanders? To just back out and say I didn't want to do it would make everyone hate me.

There was only one solution. I'd have to be sick. Sick for a few days. Sick through Monday. Long enough for them to give up on me and go back to Hollywood.

I let out a loud practice cough.

Not bad.

Then I lay back against the pillow and watched the sun come up. It looked as though it was going to be a beautiful day to develop the flu.

The next day was Thursday, and I set the stage for my "flu" attack two or three times during the day. During second period, I coughed so much the teacher asked me twice if I wanted to be excused to go get some water.

"Thank you," I managed weakly, trying to sound hoarse.

Since I hadn't slept, my eyes looked a little heavy-lidded, and that helped, too.

At lunch, I dropped my head dramatically a couple of times and rested it on my hand, as though I were having a sudden spell or something.

"Are you all right?" Elizabeth asked me anxiously.

I nodded bravely. "I'm fine. I just have a headache. That's all." *Which will turn into full-blown flu by tomorrow*, I thought to myself.

Mandy frowned. "What about the thrift shop? Do you feel well enough to go this afternoon? I have a doctor's appointment, so I'll be a little late. No one could cover for me, and I figured you'd be OK alone for a little while. Clara's niece is right next door."

"Gosh." I grimaced. "I don't know. Isn't there anybody else who could go?"

"Not me," Jessica said. "I've got to go pick up the paint from the paint store. Five cans. That means I'm going to need a couple of people to help me carry it. You guys heard Mr. Clark. I don't think we'd better put this paint job off any longer."

"I'd help, but I've got a staff meeting of the *7 & 8 Gazette* this afternoon," Elizabeth said with a worried frown.

I lifted my head and forced a smile. "I'll go, Mandy. Don't worry. I'll be fine."

Mandy's face broke into a relieved smile. "I'll come just as soon as I leave the doctor's office. By four at the latest. And maybe Evie can miss her lesson today and help out at the store. Then you could go home as soon as I get there."

"Take your time," I said quickly. "Really. Don't hurry. If I don't feel well, I'll just sit down in one of the chairs." Now I felt terrible. I sure didn't want Mandy to feel rushed at her doctor's appointment. Mandy had cancer last year. She's fine now. But she has to have regular checkups to be sure it hasn't come back. And let me tell you, you've never truly known what it feels like to be a rat until you've faked being sick and gotten sympathy from somebody who's been sick for real.

I felt so ratty, I almost looked behind me to see if I had a tail.

Luckily, there was almost no business that afternoon at the thrift shop. Most of the kids who wanted thrift-store clothes had been in the previous day. And it was sort of rainy, so there wasn't much walk-in traffic from the other shops along the street.

I decided to use the privacy to practice my lines for the phone call I was going to have with Tom Sanders tonight. His assistant, Phil, had called yesterday to say Tom would probably call me this evening to confirm times and everything.

"I'm sorry," I rasped, "but you'll have to find another actress for the part. My voice is just gone."

It wasn't bad, but it was a little over the top to be convincing. I needed to bring it down a little.

"I'm sorry," I tried again. "But my voice is going. I can tell I'm getting the flu. I might be in bed for days. I feel awful about it, but I'm afraid you'll have to find another actress to do my scene. . . . What? . . . Yes, well, I'm sorry there's no one else here in Sweet Valley *(cough cough)*. I guess you'll have to shoot it in the studio when you get back to Hollywood. I know the kids will be disappointed and I can't tell you how terrible I feel about it all."

Hmmmmm. Still too hammy.

I stood up and rolled my head around on my neck. Then I rolled my shoulders forward and backward. I thought for a moment. There are a lot of relaxation techniques that actresses use to get their posture and voice to sound more relaxed and natural.

One of them is singing the lines a few times first.

I threw back my head, opened my mouth, and belted out in my biggest soprano: *"I'm so terribly sorry, Tom, but I can't possibly do the part. My voice is gooooonnnnnne."* On the word *gone* I worked my way up the scale and then held the last note on a high C.

"Is that so?" a voice behind me commented dryly.

I whirled around and gasped in shock when I saw Evie standing behind me.

"How long have you been standing there?" I demanded.

"Long enough to figure out what's going on. You're going to back out, aren't you?" Her face kind of collapsed, like she couldn't decide whether to cry or yell. "I can't believe you're going to quit," she wailed. "Why? Why would you do something like that?"

"Evie," I began, sighing and looking straight at her.

But she turned her back, as if she didn't want to even look at me.

"Evie, listen to me," I demanded, reaching out and turning her toward me.

She tried not to look at me. "You have to listen to me," I hissed. "You have to understand. I can't do that part. I can't—" I started to say what was really on my mind. That I couldn't act anymore.

But something stopped me. I just couldn't bring myself to say it. Couldn't make the words come out of my mouth.

Pretty stupid, huh? But I guess there's some silly part of us that makes people like me want to get up in front of an audience and sing and dance and be the center of attention. And that is the same part that won't let people like me admit it when we can't do it anymore.

I couldn't tell Evie the truth. I just couldn't. So I lied. I lifted my chin as I'd seen plenty of prima donnas do and said in a really snotty tone, "I've been giving it a lot of thought, and the part's not right for me. I just don't think I am the best actress for the part."

Evie glared at me through narrowed eyes. "I can't believe you. You're just like everybody else in Hollywood. You don't care about anybody or anything important. All you care about is yourself— and what people think of you. Look how many people you're letting down. The kids at the Center. The kids at school, who are expecting to be in a movie. The Unicorns." Her eyes were snapping now. "Well, I'm glad you're quitting. I'm glad you won't be in that movie, because you're not an actress *and you never were,*" she finished with a shout. *"You were just a spoiled brat with a big toothy smile and a limo."*

And with that, Evie picked up her violin case and ran out of the store.

She slammed the door, which set the little bell on the door tinkling, its tinny sound echoing in my ears. A little, lonely sound. Like a tear in the air.

I realized then that my knees were shaking, and I collapsed into one of the chairs. Everything she'd said was true, and I felt sick. Sick to death and ashamed. The kind of sick and ashamed feeling that makes you wish you'd never been born.

Just then, Mandy came breezing in, looking fit as a fiddle. Obviously, her doctor's visit had gone fine. But when she saw me, she skidded to a stop. "You look awful," she said. "Get out of here. Go home. Take some aspirin. Drink some juice. You've got a big day coming up on Monday."

"Will you be OK here?" I asked.

"Sure," Mandy said. "Mary promised to come over after she helps with the paint. She won't be long. And Clara's niece is right next door."

I nodded and stood. "Thanks," I said hoarsely, heading for the door. I was glad that Mandy couldn't see the tears streaming down my cheeks.

"Maria!" There was a soft knock, and then Mom came in quietly.

It was the third time Mom had come up to check on me. I'd come right home from the store, announced that I had the flu, and gone straight up to my room.

Then I put on my nightgown, got into bed, and sobbed until my head hurt so much and my eyes were so swollen I really did look like I had the flu.

"Elizabeth's on the phone," Mom said in a soft voice.

I shook my head. "I don't want to talk to anybody," I answered miserably. "Nobody at all. OK? And if anybody asks, I won't be going to school tomorrow." I hadn't heard from Tom Sanders yet. I just didn't have the nerve to talk to him. I hoped he wouldn't call until tomorrow—when I felt "better."

Mom tucked the covers up around me and put her hand on my forehead. "No fever," she muttered, almost to herself.

I let out a loud groan. And then I coughed.

Mom shook her head. "We'll see how you feel in the morning," she murmured.

Ten

On Friday morning it was a little harder to look as convincingly sick. I had cried myself out by about seven the night before, and by then I was so tired from crying, I wound up sleeping all night.

All in all, I looked pretty terrific when I woke up. It took a lot of work to make Mom believe that I was sick.

"But Maria," she insisted, "you have no fever. You're not stuffed up. Whatever you had is gone. Now, get up and get dressed. And be sure you call Tom Sanders today. He called you twice last night."

"Mom, I still don't feel good."

"If you start to feel sick again at school, I'll come get you," Mom promised. "Now, come on. Get moving or you'll be late."

I stood, then sort of let my knees buckle so that I stumbled back against the bed.

"Maria!" Mom cried. "Are you all right?"

"Just a little dizzy," I said softly.

"That does it," Mom said. "I'm calling the doctor. You may not have a fever, but if you're feeling faint, something is definitely wrong."

"*No!*" I yelled.

Mom turned, startled by my loud voice.

I coughed. "No," I croaked again, trying to make my voice sound weak. "I don't think this is the kind of thing I need to see a doctor about. I think this is the kind of thing that just needs a few days in bed and quiet. Absolute quiet."

Mom put her hands on her hips and cocked one eyebrow almost up to her hairline. That face usually means Mom smells a rat but can't prove anything.

"Absolute quiet, hmm?"

I nodded.

"That means no phone calls at all?"

I nodded.

"And what if Mr. Sanders calls? Aren't you scheduled to do a shoot for him Monday? Don't you think he wants to talk to you about it?"

"Tell him I'm too sick to talk," I said in a failing voice. "And tell him I'll probably be sick for several days. This kind of thing tends to hang on. Sooo . . . I guess you'd better also tell him to plan to go back to Hollywood and shoot my scene in a studio with another actress."

I dropped my gaze so I wouldn't have to meet my mom's. She's very into honesty and telling the truth and following through on your promises. She wouldn't understand what I was doing. She'd think it was wrong.

Mom's skeptical expression disappeared and was replaced by a look of worried concern. She came over and sat down on the edge of the bed. "Maria," she said, taking my hand. "Maria, honey, what's going on here?

Mom's face looked so kind and so sympathetic, I wished I could tell her the truth. But I couldn't. I couldn't bring myself to talk about it. So I just lay back against the pillows and turned my face away. "Nothing. Just tell Tom Sanders to get another actress," I repeated.

Mom let go of my hand and put it down on the edge of the bed. "No. I won't," she said in a firm voice. "You're a child, but you're also a professional. You have an agreement with him. If he calls again, you'll have to cancel out on him yourself."

I heard Mom leave the room and close the door. The sound was something between a firm slam and a snap.

Mom was on to me. No doubt about it. She knew something was going on. She just didn't know what.

But at least she wasn't going to force me to go to school. I turned over on my stomach and buried my head in my pillow, debating with myself over whether I wanted to cry some more—or just lie there wishing I were dead.

By that afternoon, I really was sick. You know, I think I learned something that day about staying healthy. Sure, smoking will make you sick. Drinking will make you sick. Drugs will make you sick. Too much sun can make you sick. And green fruit will make you sick.

Know what else makes you sick? Head-pounding gut-churning crawl-in-a-hole-and-die sick?

Guilt.

I'm serious. By four that afternoon (after refusing to go to the phone every time it rang for me), I felt as sick as I'd ever felt in my whole life. My head felt like somebody was standing behind me and whacking my skull with a sledgehammer, and my stomach lurched dangerously.

There were so many people I was letting down, I was having a hard time keeping track of them.

Let's see . . . Evie had done a pretty good job of listing them. First were the kids at the Center and their families. Plus Mrs. Willard and the staff. Tom Sanders. (He'd live. He'd just think I was a primo welcher, that's all.) Then there were all the kids who expected Tom Sanders to bring his camera crew to Sweet Valley Middle School so they could be in a movie. The Unicorns. From what Janet had told me, I had already sunk pretty low on the drama staff's list. This stunt would shoot me right to the bottom.

Nina would think I was a total coward. My dad would *really* read me the riot act. (He's very big on keeping your promises, too—especially when they relate to business.) My mom would be disappointed in me, but she'd still love me. She'd probably be the only one, though.

I groaned and rolled over. There was only one solution.

Tomorrow, I was going to have to run away from

Sweet Valley and live someplace else under an assumed name. Probably become a street kid. I'd never get an education, and I'd spend my life flipping hamburgers somewhere.

I groaned again. And between feeling guilty and thinking about greasy hamburgers, I felt even sicker.

Eleven

I spent most of Friday evening leaning back against my pillows, listlessly flipping through the pages of a beauty magazine. I was still avoiding the phone, and I hadn't spoken to anybody all day. Mom had refused to do my dirty work for me—but she was taking messages, and I had quite a little stack of them by my bed. Tom Sanders. Elizabeth. Mandy. Every time I looked at them, it made me even more miserable.

And aside from feeling miserable, I was bored out of my skull. So bored, I actually went into the bathroom, which was just off my room, and followed the magazine's "easy-to-mix-at-home" facial mask recipe.

It turned out sort of hard and grainy and sticky. I was in the bathroom, trying to wash it off, when I heard Mom come into my room.

I stuck my head out of the bathroom. "Looking for me?"

"Your friends are here," Mom said in a very neutral voice.

"Which friends?" I asked.

"All of them, " Mom answered. Then she backed
out the door.

The next thing I knew, the Unicorns were filing
in—*led by Evie!*

My room's not that big, so by the time Elizabeth,
Jessica, Mandy, Ellen, Lila, Evie, and Mary came in
and found places, it was pretty crowded.

I got back in my spot—the middle of my bed—and
most of the Unicorns sat at the edges or at the end. I
do have a small overstuffed armchair and footstool in
my room, and Elizabeth and Jessica sat on those.

There was a long, long silence, and I began to feel
a little sweaty—and incredibly embarrassed that my
face was still covered with the remains of the mask:
big patches of hard, grainy gunk.

"Is that some kind of new flu remedy?" Mandy
asked in a tone I couldn't read. It was too neutral. I
couldn't tell if she was being serious or sarcastic.

In fact, I wasn't quite sure why they were here.
Because they thought I was sick and needed a visit?
Or because they had figured out the truth?

I couldn't tell from their faces. Elizabeth and Mary
looked concerned. Jessica and Lila looked really mad.
Everybody else just looked noncommittal.

Finally, Evie broke the silence.

"I'm sorry," she said immediately. "For two things.
Maria, I'm sorry for blowing up at you at the shop. I
wish I could take back the things I said, because after
I calmed down, I realized you'd never go back on

your word for no reason. There had to be something going on I didn't understand."

"So she came to me and Elizabeth," Jessica said flatly. "She asked us if we knew if you had any reason to fake being sick to get out of the shoot. We said we couldn't think of a reason in the world. And furthermore, nobody but a huge creep would do something like that."

"Jessica!" Elizabeth warned.

"Well, come on, Lizzie. She wasn't at school today, and Tom Sanders called *our* house this afternoon in a panic because he couldn't get Maria on the phone. What was I supposed to think? Huh?"

"You were at home this afternoon?" Elizabeth asked with a frown. "What about the paint? After you guys got 'stuck' at the mall and couldn't pick it up yesterday, I thought you talked Mom into going to the paint store with you this afternoon."

"Paint! Paint! Paint! Is that all you ever think about?" Jessica practically shouted.

"Well, when are *you* going to think about it?" Elizabeth retorted.

"You told Mr. Clark we'd have it done in time for the shoot," Ellen pointed out.

"Yeah," Mary added. She looked around the room. "We should never have put Jessica in charge of this," she said.

"For your information," Jessica said huffily, "my mother is picking up the paint now—as we speak. And she's storing it in our garage. I talked to Mr. Peters, and he'll be at school tomorrow until one o'clock. We can meet at my house at eleven, get the paint, and be finished by one o'clock. So there."

Everybody broke into a grin.

"Way to go, Jessica," Mandy said.

Meanwhile, Evie's head was snapping from person to person during this whole conversation, as though she couldn't believe we were actually wasting time talking about something so stupid. "Would you guys please quit talking about paint?"

"Sorry," the Unicorns all muttered. Then they all turned their attention back to me. There was a long awkward pause and rustling as everybody settled themselves to resume the discussion.

Evie held up her hands again. "The second thing I want to apologize for is going behind your back to your friends. But when I saw all of you together and how close you were, I realized that if one of your friends was in some kind of trouble, you would want the others to know—so you could all go and help them. And *they* would want to know if *you* had a problem, so they could come and help you."

She looked around the room, as if she still wasn't sure she had done the right thing.

Just then I wanted to slug her. Why couldn't she mind her own business? I did have a problem. OK. But that didn't mean I wanted all my friends sitting on my bed, staring at me with angry, skeptical, and concerned faces.

So I just slumped down and pulled the covers over my head. "I have the flu," I said in a stuffed-up, quiet voice. "My voice is almost completely gone. I feel weak and tired. If Evie thinks I'm faking, she simply misunderstood and—"

"Brad!" I heard Ellen say. There were loud footsteps on the stairs.

Four of the girls jumped off the bed and crowded around the door.

"Thank you for coming," I heard Jessica gush into the hallway. "Please come talk some sense into her. She's right over here on the bed."

Suddenly, I remembered the clinging mask that was still stuck all over my face—plus the plastic clips that were in my hair and the sour taste in my mouth from only eating toast and tea (flu food) all day.

The thought of facing Brad Marshall like this was more than I could stand. So I sat straight up, glared at my friends so hard I thought sparks would come out of my eyes, and pointed my finger dangerously. *"If you think for a second I will let you bring him in here with me looking like this, you're all crazy!"* I thundered. *"Make him stay downstairs. I'll be down in a minute."*

Then I threw back the covers and practically flew out of bed toward the bathroom, where I knew my makeup case was waiting.

I was halfway there before I heard the roar of laughter behind me. I turned around and saw the knot of girls in the doorway part to reveal—nobody.

There wasn't a soul standing there. They'd tricked me.

"So your voice is gone?" Ellen asked with a giggle.

"And you're too weak to get out of bed," Elizabeth commented.

I hung my head and stood there. I was caught. I couldn't go back to playing sick now.

Jessica crossed her arms over her chest in disgust. She sat back down and shrugged. "So would you please tell us what's going on?"

I shook my head. I had no explanation.

Elizabeth stood and put her hand on Evie's shoulder. "You know what, Evie? I think you did absolutely the right thing by coming to us. But I think this is something she doesn't want to share with us. And I don't think we can force her to."

"But this isn't just about Maria," Mandy countered in a matter-of-fact voice. "We promised the Center a new roof. *We* did. Not just Maria. The Unicorn Club. If she reneges on this deal, so do all of us. She said it herself to Mrs. Willard. She was the ambassador of the Unicorn Club."

"I'm with Elizabeth," Ellen squeaked, which surprised me. Ellen usually waits to see which way the group is going before she makes up her mind. I guess you could say she's kind of indecisive. "We may be a club. But that doesn't give us the right to stick our noses into one another's business."

"But Maria made it our business when she involved the school, the club, and the Center," Mary argued reasonably.

They were right. All of them were right. Friends could be friends and still have a right to privacy now and then. But I had made a promise as a Unicorn. And if I broke that promise, a lot of people were going to be unhappy. And not just unhappy with me—unhappy with the whole group.

"Won't you please talk to us?" Elizabeth begged in a soft voice. "Tell us why you don't want to do the part? How can we help you with a problem if we don't know what it is?"

I reached for my flannel robe and pulled it on, cinching the belt tight. For some reason that little gesture always seems to give me a little confidence when I'm about to face something unpleasant. I think I got it from watching old Bette Davis movies. "I can't act anymore," I said in a soft voice.

"What did she say?" Ellen asked from the back.

I yanked the ends of my belt again and lifted my chin. "I said I can't act anymore," I blurted out in a defiant voice. "And I'm afraid."

"Afraid of what?" Elizabeth asked softly.

"Of making a fool of myself in front of the whole school. Of having to do take after take after take because I keep flubbing my lines or because my acting is just so stinky."

Elizabeth's brow furrowed, as though she was trying hard to understand. "But what makes you think you can't act anymore?"

I looked all around the room. Curiosity and disbelief were written on every face.

"Because . . ." I began. "Because . . . because I can't." Then I threw myself facedown on the bed and began to cry.

"What's going on here?" came a deep voice from the hallway.

We all turned and saw Clara, Evie's grandmother, standing in the doorway.

"Grandma!" Evie cried, running toward her. Clara scooped her up in a hug and then gazed curiously around the room.

"I just got in from New York," Clara explained. "And I came over here because Evie left me a note that said she was at the Slaters' and that there was an emergency." Clara sat down next to me on the bed, tipped my face upward, and examined it with a professional eye. "I'd say that *is* an emergency. Don't you shoot Monday? Somebody get a dermatologist. Quick."

I sat up and laughed. Then I peeled off some of the mask. "The emergency has nothing to do with my skin. It's that I don't want—I *can't*," I corrected quickly, "do the shoot Monday. Because I can't act anymore."

"What makes you think you can't act anymore?" Clara demanded.

I swallowed. "A whole bunch of things. But mostly because a friend of mine in the drama department told me I didn't get the lead in the new play."

Clara threw back her head and laughed deeply and richly. "Is that all? Don't be ridiculous. You will always, always, always, *always* be turned down for more parts than you will get. It's the nature of the acting profession. Always has been. Always will be."

She got off the bed and went over and made Jessica give up her place in the armchair. Then she sat down with an amused sigh and propped her elegant chin up with her hands. "Getting parts has nothing to do with your acting talent. You must learn that right away. Don't let others tell you you're a good or bad actress. That determination can only come from you. So Maria, you decide and tell me: are you a good actress or not?"

I sat in the middle of my bed, thinking about it for a long time.

"You know what?" I said finally. "I don't know anymore. This scene I'm supposed to do is so different from anything I've ever done, I just don't know if I'm a good enough actress to pull it off."

Clara shrugged, as if it wasn't very important. "So one way or the other, on Monday you will learn something. That means it won't be a wasted day."

"But what if I'm terrible?"

Mandy put her hand on my shoulder. "That's where we come in. We'll be behind you all the way. And even if you bomb, we'll still be your biggest fans."

I looked around at all the smiling and affectionate faces and immediately felt better. Of course they wouldn't abandon me if I was no good.

I had been judging my Sweet Valley friends by the standards of Hollywood. There you're only as good as your last hit. And they're only nice to you if you're a big success. Or if you have the right clothes or hair or car.

The Unicorns were way beyond that. They were true friends, through thick and thin. *A good club is a club that brings out the best in its members and not the worst,* Mandy was always reminding us.

I felt a little glow of pride creep over me. I belonged to a good club. These girls were getting me up, out of my bed, and ready to do something I was petrified to do.

But I'd do it. I'd do it for them.

Twelve

Clank!

"*Ouch!*"

"Shhhhhhh," everybody chorused.

"You just ran right into my back with that bucket," Jessica whispered irritably. "Watch where you're going."

"How? It's hardly light yet," Ellen complained, moving clumsily step up the front steps, doing her best to carry a heavy bucket of paint.

Clank! went the can as it tapped the back of Jessica's ankle.

"Ow!"

"Shhhhh," warned Mary.

"I'm cold," Ellen said.

"Would you quit complaining?" Jessica spat.

Slam! went the bucket as Ellen dropped it on the ground. "Why shouldn't I complain? You told us everything was all set for us to do this Saturday. But then Saturday rolls around and nobody can find you. There's nobody at your house, so we can't get into your garage to get the paint. And you don't show up until four that afternoon, when Mr. Peters is gone and the building is locked. So now, instead of getting a good sleep on an important morning, we have to sneak into school to do what we could have walked right in and done legally on Saturday."

"Yeah!" muttered several voices.

It was a long speech for Ellen, and she was absolutely right. Jessica had done a complete fade on Saturday. Reason? She and Lila had finagled appointments with some big-deal hairdresser at the Valley Mall, but only if they could come right away. They hadn't gotten back in time to paint the lockers.

Jessica gave us all that grin that makes us forgive her for being such a jerk sometimes. Then she shook her hair, which had been transformed into a mass of gentle curls. "Lila and I didn't mean to be late. But the stylist—his name is Edge, isn't that the coolest?— was late and we couldn't get back in time. You guys aren't *that* mad, are you?"

"*Yes!*" Everybody practically screamed in a whisper.

It was five o'clock on Monday morning, and we were all tiptoeing into school to paint the bank of lockers. Mr. Clark had taken Jessica aside on Friday and said very firmly that if the lockers were not painted in time for the shoot this morning, every single Unicorn would be on probation and it would be the last—repeat, *last*—time he would ever give his permission for something like this inside the school, no matter how good the cause.

Thanks to Jessica, we'd blown our chance to get it done on Saturday. On Sunday, everybody had had chores or homework or some kind of family commitment. And besides, Mr. Peters had said he couldn't open the school building for us on Sunday. He'd refused to open it up early for us today, too. School policy forbade students from being inside the school before seven A.M., for security reasons.

So now here we were, having to sneak in at five A.M. on a Monday morning.

We found an unlocked window that led to the first-floor science room. I pushed it open, then I boosted Jessica in. Then the two of us leaned out and pulled Ellen up. Then came Mandy and Mary. Lila. Elizabeth. And finally, Evie. (She had insisted on helping.) Along with all our junk.

Once inside, we took a little bit of time to sort everything out. Aside from flashlights, drop cloths, rollers, brushes, and pans, and five big cans of industrial paint with brown wrappers around them, each girl also had her own duffel bag full of the clothes she was planning to wear for the movie, plus makeup and everything else we would need to get ready for school.

"OK," Jessica said, swinging her duffel bag over her shoulder and hoisting a can in one hand. She held a flashlight in the other hand. "Let's get moving. We've got to be finished by seven, at least. That's when the doors open. First bell is at eight, and the shoot is at nine."

We all nodded, reached for some gear, and followed Jessica out of the science room and into the South Hall, where the long bank of central lockers stood.

Frankly, I had gotten so used to seeing that long purple stripe down the middle of the locker bank, it didn't bother me. But it bothered Mr. Clark big-time.

"OK," Jessica was saying. "Everybody with a can, shake it."

So of course every single person began to shake their hips and sing.

"Knock it off," Jessica huffed, then giggled. "I meant everybody with a *paint* can."

"Ohhhhhhhhhh," Ellen, Mary, and Lila all cried innocently. "Why didn't you say so?"

"Shhhh," Elizabeth warned us again. "We're not supposed to be here."

Jessica had spread out a bunch of newspapers on the floor. Then she picked up one of the large cans, shook it hard, and put it on top of the newspaper. "Now, you open it like this," she said, reaching for a wooden spatula.

She wedged it under the lip of the can and pried the top off. But when she pulled off the lid, the smile on her face disappeared and her eyes bulged.

Quickly, she rubbed them hard, blinked several times, and then looked closer. With just the light from the flashlight, it was pretty dim. "Turn the lights on, somebody."

Ellen ran and hit the switch on all the big overhead lights.

Jessica let out a loud groan. "Ohhh noooo."

"What's wrong?" we all asked.

Jessica lifted her head and crooked her finger, signaling us all to come and take a look.

Slowly, we all gathered around.

"Wow!" Mary said.

Ellen just whistled.

The paint was *pink*. I'm not talking slightly pink, pale pink, or blush.

I'm talking real pink, prom-dress pink, electric pink, candy-heart pink.

"What color did you order?" Mary demanded.

"Industrial Pink," Jessica answered with a shaking voice.

Mary peeled the brown wrapper off the paint can and nodded. "Well, you got Imperial Pink."

"It wasn't my fault," Jessica said quickly. "Ellen, you were with me. You heard me order it."

Ellen nodded. "The paint store goofed up. But what can we do about it now?"

Evie picked up a brush, dipped it in the can, and delicately wiped the end against the locker surface. "I think pink is a very pretty color. I say, let's paint. Mr. Clark said he wanted the bank repainted. But he didn't say what color." She smiled wickedly. "Right?"

It took a few minutes to sink in, but when it did, we all began laughing hysterically.

"Let's do it," Jessica urged.

We were finished, cleaned up, and out of there long before the doors opened. That gave us plenty of time to stash the gear behind the woodworking shop and then nip back into the girls' room to change our clothes, brush our hair, and apply a little makeup.

I put some on, too. I knew that when the crew arrived, they'd put me in professional makeup, but still, I hated facing anybody without a little mascara and lip gloss.

We all had our thrift-store outfits on, and we lined up for inspection. Mandy gave us all a last critical look before we left the bathroom

Mandy walked up and down, like a general inspecting her troops. She had really gone all the way today. She was wearing a pair of men's paisley pajama bottoms under a short tartan kilt, with a ribbed poorboy top and a paisley scarf worn like a sash. On her head was a tam with a big pom-pom. She looked great—sort of like a punk bagpiper.

We all stood up really straight as she passed us by. Mary had on a forties vamp outfit. Flowing pants and a floaty top. Her fine blond hair lay flat all around her head in spit curls. And the only makeup she wore was dead white powder and red, red lipstick.

"Good," Mandy said approvingly, and Mary blushed with pleasure.

Lila had on a white crocheted vest over a black body suit and jeans. On her feet were saddle shoes.

Mandy smiled and shook her head. "Great."

On to Jessica. She was wearing faded jeans and a blue, pink, and purple floral-patterned vest. Underneath the vest was a white oxford shirt with the sleeves rolled up, and on her head she had a hat with a big flower pinned to the upturned brim. Elizabeth had chosen a cool fifties-style housedress, accented with colorful jewelry, patterned tights, and lace-up boots.

Evie was there, too, and she trailed behind Mandy like a second-in-command, straightening a shoulder pad or retying a tie when it was necessary.

She was very funky, too, in her patterned men's dress shirt and tie. She wore them over a stretch miniskirt and tights. Her long hair hung straight down her back, and I thought she might be the prettiest one of us all.

It didn't matter what I had on. Tom's costume department would dress me when they arrived. The drama department dressing rooms had been turned over to the movie crew to use for offices and dressing rooms. Speaking of which . . .

I looked at my watch, and my heart did a little nervous flip. "It's just about that time," I announced.

Everybody got really quiet and nodded.

"Break a leg, Maria," Elizabeth said. Then she gave me a big hug.

"We're behind you all the way," Mandy repeated.

The whole group headed back to the science room, slipped back out the window we had come through earlier, and landed on the grass with a soft thud.

Jessica was the last one out. She closed the window behind her, and then fell softly to the ground beside me.

She grinned. "Let's go around the block and then walk into school with everybody else. I want to hear what they say when they see those pink lockers."

We all burst into laughter, then we split up and decided to stagger our arrivals at school so we could look as if we were arriving separately.

Mandy and I got picked to show up last.

She looked at her watch. "We've got at least twenty minutes to kill before first bell," she said. "You can take the time to practice your lines, if you want."

I nodded and fell into step beside her. "What *do* you steal?" I asked, making my voice sound skeptical. "*What* do you steal?" I tried again, making my voice sound innocent.

I heard Mandy sigh. "If that's all I'm going to hear, it's going to be a long walk."

I threw out my arms in irritation. "Sorry," I said in a sarcastic voice. "So it's not Shakespeare. I can't help it. It's what I'm supposed to say in the movie."

Mandy grinned. "Hey! Chill out. I'm not knocking it. Shakespeare's not putting a new roof on the Center. Maria Slater is."

I shook my head and smiled.

"No. Maria Slater isn't. The Unicorns are."

By the time we got to school and went in, the hallway was packed. Just packed. I don't think there was one single absentee that day. Everybody wanted to see the movie being shot. Most people wanted to be in it. And every girl, no matter what grade, wanted a close-up look at Brad Marshall.

When I thought about him, my arms and legs started to feel like jelly, so I forced myself not to think about him.

The crowd was working its way down the hall, and then suddenly there were loud guffaws of laughter that began to filter all the way back.

I felt Mandy tug at my arm. "Come on," she said

as she tugged me through the crowd toward the front.

The crowd parted to let us through, and I saw one of the funniest sights I have ever seen in my life.

There was Mr. Clark staring down at Jessica and Jessica staring up at him with big innocent eyes. They were nose to nose in front of the locker bank, and Mr. Clark looked completely outraged.

Behind Jessica stood the rest of the Unicorns, so Mandy and I hurried to join them.

Mr. Clark was so outraged, he could hardly control his emotions. Finally, all he could do was let out one strangled word that sounded like *Pink.*

Jessica blinked innocently. "You said to have the lockers repainted by the time the movie crew arrived. We followed your instructions."

"But they're pink!" Mr. Clark finally exploded.

"My mom felt the same way about our new couch when it was first delivered," Ellen said, peeking out from behind Jessica and launching into an imitation of her mother. "You should have heard her. 'It's too big. And that color! What'll your father say?'"

We all broke up and covered our mouths with our hands. As I said before, Ellen does a great imitation of her mother. Then Ellen smiled. "But you'll get used to this, just like my mom got used to the sofa."

"I don't WANT to get used to pink lockers!" Mr. Clark thundered. But before he could say another word, there was a shout of excitement. The big movie trucks had pulled up outside, and men were starting to unload cables and lights and cameras.

Immediately, the kids started running for the windows and doors. "Now, don't get in anybody's way!" Mr. Clark boomed after them.

He turned a disgusted eye on Jessica. "We will discuss this later." He looked at me and then at his watch. "Maria, I think you'd better report to the drama rooms. Please tell Mr. Sanders that I am at his disposal. If he needs anything from me or the staff, he should let us know." He looked around and saw Evie hovering nearby. "Evie," he began, smiling, "can I appoint you special student messenger for the day? That means you must stay with the movie crew and come get me if I'm needed."

"Sure." Evie grinned. "Thanks. That sounds like fun."

She reached out and squeezed my hand. "It will be fun, Maria. Just like in the old days. Right? Me following you around."

"Right." I responded, trying hard to smile. But suddenly my lips felt like frozen rubber, and I was terrified as I returned her squeeze.

"Yikes!" she yipped.

"Oh, sorry!" I said, immediately releasing her hand. In my fear, I had clenched her hand practically hard enough to break it.

She let go of my hand and looked at me levelly. "Relax, Maria," she said. "Even if you bomb, you've still got six of the greatest friends I've ever seen. If I ever become jealous of you for anything, it won't be your looks or your stardom or your money—it'll be your friends."

"Miss Slater!" called an imperious voice. "We're ready for you."

I turned and saw the makeup and wardrobe people beckoning me.

"Break a leg," Evie whispered. Then she pushed
me in their direction.

Thirteen

Beads of sweat were rolling down my forehead and temples. Somebody from makeup stepped forward and quickly blotted them. It was taking forever to get the lights right. Forever.

All around me, I could hear an impatient murmur coming from the students. Nobody ever realizes how much time it takes to set up a shot. I could tell that they were getting restless, and I even heard a few kids complain. I smiled. First-time extras always behave that way.

"Love the pink lockers," Tom Sanders was saying. "Great touch, somebody. Thanks."

He was blocking the scene with me and Brad, and we were standing in front of the freshly painted lockers. Blocking means figuring who's going to stand where, say what, and walk in what direction. It's a dry run, basically. Not a rehearsal or anything like that.

We'd been over the blocking about four times now, so I felt fairly confident about where I was supposed to be in the scene. I wouldn't have minded rehearsing the scene, but Tom Sanders said he hated rehearsing. He said it spoiled the spontaneity. "If you know your lines, you'll find the moment," he said to me seriously.

My stomach was so tight with nervousness I couldn't even answer. I felt as if I needed to rehearse. But I knew time was ticking away. The crews belonged to a union, which meant they had strict rules about how long they would work and how much they would get paid for overtime.

I looked up at the clock and wanted to cry. If we didn't get started, we weren't going to have time for more than about two takes. I felt so stiff and frightened, I knew it was going to take me two takes just to warm up.

Suddenly, a beam of light hit me right in the face.

"We've got it now, Tom," said a female voice from somewhere in the background.

There was a sudden flurry of activity as Tom yelled, "Places!"

I found my place in front of the lockers.

Stop, I wanted to yell. *Stop, I'm not ready.*

But it was too late.

"Rolling!" yelled Tom.

"Locker Thief, take one!" barked the man with the clapper.

Click! went the clapper.

I took some deep breaths and then I heard it, a sound I'd just about forgotten. It was the almost silent whirring of a camera. Something about that sound brought it all back to me. And suddenly my heart was pounding with excitement. I wasn't really me anymore. Maria Slater was slipping away, and I was becoming the shy, ditsy seventh-grader I was playing. It was like being in a dream. I was there, but in a way I wasn't there.

I felt my face fall into the slightly vacant expression of somebody you have to explain jokes to but love anyway. I kind of bopped down the hall as if listening to some private hip-hop in my head. Dimly, I was aware of a camera tracking around me to shoot from the front.

Then reality slipped away. And I was into it.

"Becky!"

I stopped and turned around when I heard my name.

Then my mouth fell open. I couldn't believe it. The greatest-looking boy in the world was smiling at me. Me. Becky McGillan. School nerd.

He moved a little closer. A little too close. He was making me nervous. So I backed up toward the lockers. Boys didn't usually pay too much attention to Becky McGillan. He must want something. I was glad my lunch money was safely tucked in the heel of my tennis shoe.

"Do you know me?" he asked softly, a teasing smile on his lips.

I shook my head. "I don't think so." Then I squinted through my glasses. "You're not in my biology class, are you?"

The boy laughed. "I'm the thief."

I made my eyes bug comically and pressed my

back against my locker, as if to protect my belongings. "What do you steal?" I asked in a nervous voice.

"Hearts," the boy answered, leaning closer. "And kisses," he added, brushing his lips against mine.

Then he turned and walked away, slowly, down the long length of the hall.

I was coming out of it now. It's like waking up. We'd played the scene and it was almost over. I'd seen the story board, and I had one more reaction shot. I had to keep the grin from creeping onto my face. Hammy or not, I was going for laughs.

I saw the camera pan back in my direction, and as soon as I was sure it was in position, I began to flutter my lashes. I turned my eyes upward and swooned back against the locker.

"Ooops!" I heard a familiar voice cry.

The next thing I knew, Jessica had jumped into the scene and slapped a WET PAINT sign on the locker next to my head. Before I could respond, she had jackrabbitted out of the scene.

Tom made a rolling gesture with his hands. He wanted us to stay in character and keep going with the scene.

I stayed in character and struggled for balance on wobbly legs. Then I pushed my glasses to the bridge of my nose and tried to walk with some vestige of dignity down the hall, with pink paint slathered all over my back.

I walked the length of the hall as if in a daze, then turned the corner.

"Cut!" I heard Tom yell.

I came running back around the corner just in time to collide with Tom. He threw his arms around me and lifted me off my feet. "Perfect. Beautiful. Got it in one take." He happily pinched my cheek. "I knew I'd get the best from *the* Maria Slater."

Then he looked over and saw Jessica. "You!" he said.

Jessica stepped behind Mary. "I'm sorry. I'm sorry."

Tom Sanders threw back his head and laughed. "Sorry, nothing. It was a great comic touch. It'll stay in."

"You mean I'll be in the scene with Maria?"

Tom nodded.

All the Unicorns began to cheer.

Tom kissed my cheek, and then Brad came over and shook my hand. "You were really terrific," he said. "I hope we can work together again."

All I could do was nod. OK, so I'm an actress. That doesn't mean I can't be star-struck, too.

Tom broke away and began clapping his hands loudly over his head. "Attention, people. Attention, people. You all look great, so get ready. We're going to shoot some crowd scenes now."

He pointed to several poeple holding clipboards and wearing jackets that said SECONDHAND ROSE on them.

"The people in the jackets are production assistants. They'll show you what to do. So I want you to break up into groups. They'll give you the rundown on what we need."

Mandy, who happened to be standing right near us, plucked at my sleeve. "See those jackets," she hissed. "Those are the kind of jackets we need for the Unicorn Club."

Tom turned and grinned at Mandy. "You like those jackets?"

Mandy nodded. "Our club's going to get matching jackets like those just as soon as we save some money."

"Tom!" one of the cameramen yelled. "We need you over here."

Tom excused himself and took off toward the man. "On my way," he said briskly.

Tom was as good as his word. I had a check in my hand by four that afternoon when the movie trucks rolled away. Tom tore the check off and threw the checkbook back on the seat of his car. Then he kissed my cheek. "Thanks, Maria. You're a good actress. Look me up when you come back to Hollywood."

Then he kissed every single Unicorn. When he got to Mandy, he studied her face for a moment. "You're a talented girl," he said sincerely. "We couldn't have gotten everybody looking right without you. If you do decide to become a costume designer and I can ever do anything to help you, just let me know." He handed her his card, and Mandy smiled proudly.

Tom climbed into his sports car and revved the engine. "'Bye, Unicorns," he shouted, pulling out into the street and passing the lumbering line of trucks and trailers that were slowly moving in a line—back to Hollywood.

"'Bye!" we all chorused.

Then, as soon as he was around the corner, everyone began grabbing at the check. How much was it? Would it be enough?

I grinned as it was passed from hand to hand. "More than enough," I answered.

"Come on," Jessica urged. "Let's run over to the Center. Maybe Mrs. Willard is there and Maria can show it to her right now."

"Last one to the Center is a rotten actress," I yelled, taking off at top speed.

Behind me, I could hear the other Unicorns shrieking and laughing, and they chased me all ten blocks.

Fourteen

Things were so busy for everybody that a week went by before we were able to hold our next Unicorn meeting. This time, we decided to hold it at school in the art room, since Mary and Ellen needed to spend the rest of the afternoon in the library and I had an appointment with the drama coach just before school was over.

I was the last to arrive, and Elizabeth grinned and moved down a place so I could sit between her and Jessica.

Now that we were all assembled, Mandy went to the front table, knocked on it with her knuckle, and called the meeting to order.

"Since I left the minutes book at home," she began, grinning sheepishly, "I'll skip the formal reading of the minutes and just remind everybody that last week was a total blast. The Unicorn rep is solid as granite now that we've managed to actually get a movie shot here in our very own middle school *and* buy a new roof for the day-care center."

We all grinned at one another and pumped our fists victoriously.

Mandy reached into her vest pocket. "As president of the club, I've received two letters addressed to all of us, which I would like to read out loud."

She cleared her throat.

> Dear Unicorns,
>
> The work on the roof is progressing nicely, and I've notified all our families that they can begin bringing the kids back starting next week. They all send their thanks and undying gratitude to the Unicorns, and especially to Maria, whose hard work and talent made the new roof possible.
>
> Needless to say, I send mine along with theirs. Girls, I truly do not know what we would have done without your help. And if you ever decide to change the name of your club, you might consider calling yourselves Angels instead of Unicorns.
>
> Again, many thanks,
> Mrs. Nancy Willard
> Executive Director
> Sweet Valley Child Care Center

We all high-fived each other and whistled, and a bunch of people patted me on the back.

Mandy pulled another note from her vest pocket. "This one is from Mrs. Kim."

> Dear Unicorns,

Thank you for taking such good care of my shop while I was away. You girls are born merchandisers, and I was so pleased with the amount I found in the cash drawer, I am sending you double our agreed-upon fee.

Thanks again,
Clara Kim

Mandy held up the check and read out the amount. "That'll cover the paint," Jessica said happily.

"But what about the toupee?" Ellen squeaked. "We still owe Mr. Clark for his toupee."

"How about if we just tell him he looks better without it?" Ellen said.

"How about if *you* tell him?" Jessica suggested, drawing hoots and laughs from everybody.

"Why don't we draw straws to see who tells him?" Mary suggested with a guffaw.

"Order!" Mandy yelled. "Order!"

Sheepishly, we all quieted down.

Mandy looked around the room. "Whether or not he looks better without his toupee is beside the point. Fair's fair. We still owe Mr. Clark some money, and we're just going to have to figure out some way to pay him back. But I suggest we table that problem for the next meeting. Everybody's in kind of a hurry today, and we have more important business to discuss."

"We do?" Jessica exclaimed, sitting up straighter in her seat.

Mandy nodded and I grinned. Mandy had let me in on the secret, and I had a role to play when the time came.

Mandy leaned under the table and hoisted up a huge box, which she plopped down on one of the long tables.

"What's that?" Ellen asked.

Mandy whipped the top off the box, dove down into it, and fished up the coolest purple satin jacket you've ever seen. When she turned it around to show the back, we all gasped. The word *Unicorns* was written across the back in white script letters. "Our club jackets," Mandy explained.

Everybody was squealing and gasping, and Mandy held up her hands for quiet. "Listen." She held up a note Tom Sanders had written her.

Dear Mandy,

Thanks millions for your help costuming *Secondhand Rose.* I've seen the rushes, and I can tell already we've got a hit on our hands. I know the Unicorns played a big part in getting everybody psyched and ready, so I want to express my appreciation with these jackets. Enjoy!

Live long and prosper,
Tom Sanders

That was it. There was no holding us back. Everybody rushed to the box and began pulling out jackets until they found the one with their name sewn in white script on the front.

After a few minutes, everybody was satisfied. Ellen's fit her perfectly. Lila's had an elegant flare in the back. Elizabeth's was a little snug, and Jessica's had a funky bagginess to it. Mine fit just right—not too big, not too small. And Mandy's was huge, which suited her fine.

It wasn't until everybody had found their jacket that Mary noticed one more jacket in the box. "Hey," she said. "There's one too many. And it's got a little patch sewn over where the name should be."

"We'll use it as an extra," Jessica said, beginning to put the top back on the box.

But Mandy stopped her. "That jacket gives me an idea," she said in a serious voice.

We all looked at her. She looked a little nervous. But she seemed prepared to hold her ground.

"What's your idea?" Lila asked impatiently.

"I think even numbers are luckier than odd ones," Mandy said. "And I'd be a lot happier if there were eight girls in the club instead of seven."

"Huh?" All the girls looked at one another.

"I guess what I'm trying to say is that even though we're a committed club, and we think we work well together, this time we almost blew it. An outsider got us together on a problem and helped us solve it. Evie. Without Evie, we would never have known what Maria's real problem was—or how to help her with it."

I stood up. "Mandy's right. And so . . . I propose that we ask Evie to become a member of the Unicorn Club."

"I second the motion," Elizabeth said quickly.

Mandy grinned her thanks at us both. "All in favor."

"Aye!" Every voice responded in unison.

The ayes had it. Mandy nodded to me and I

opened the door to the hall, where Evie was nervously waiting. She was supposed to wait for me to ask her in and formally tell her that she had been nominated for membership. But Evie came twirling into the room with a dancing step.

"I knew it!" she squealed happily. "I knew it!" She was grinning from ear to ear and practically dancing with excitement. "Yes, yes, yes, yes . . . I accept, I accept," she added.

I rolled my eyes and shook my head. "You're supposed to wait until we ask you," I managed to whisper in her ear.

But I don't think she heard a word I said, she was so excited. She just kept saying "Yes!" and hugging us as she worked her way up to the table, where she picked up the last jacket and twirled into it, never giving us a chance to say a thing. Mandy reached over and pulled a loose thread on the jacket's front. The patch fell off to reveal Evie's name sewn in white script, too.

I could tell by the expression on Lila's and Jessica's faces that they were a little bit offended and that they thought Evie was taking too much for granted. After all, they had been Unicorns since sixth grade, and the whole thing was a little sacred to them. In the old days, getting into the club had been a pretty intricate process.

But now Evie was looking at all of us as if we were the greatest friends in the whole world. Not even hard-liners like Lila and Jessica could hold on to their cold expressions. Pretty soon both girls were grinning and standing in line for the next round of hugs.

"Oh, I'm just so happy," Evie babbled. "And I know I'm the youngest Unicorn, but I'll try to act older, I mean . . . I'll try not to embarrass you all . . . oops!"—she giggled nervously—"too late for that. I mean, you're probably all kind of embarrassed already and—"

"*Evie!*" we all said at once.

She put her fingers nervously to her mouth and winced. "What?" she asked softly.

"*Chill!*" we all yelled.

Then we all threw our arms around one another and laughed and laughed and laughed.

"Maria!" Mr. Drew gasped. "Where would you get an idea like that? Of course I don't think you're a bad actress. Quite the reverse."

Mr. Drew is the head of the drama department, and he's always been very nice to me. When I made the appointment to meet with him, he had agreed to meet with me and also to keep whatever I told him confidential.

We were sitting in his office, which was full of cardboard boxes, half-painted pieces of scenery, and stacks of plays.

Mr. Drew took off his glasses and gave them a rigorous polish, which is usually a sign that he's upset. "I can't understand what would make you think the department had anything less than the highest regard for your abilities."

"The fact that you gave the lead in the new play to Marion Weinstein and not to me," I blurted out unhappily.

Mr. Drew put his glasses back on. "How do you know that? The roles have not been posted."

I dropped my eyes. "I heard it somewhere," I mumbled. "Is it true?"

"Yes. It's true," he said.

My eyes flew to his face. "But—"

He held up his hand, as if to stop me before I got started.

"Maria, Sweet Valley Middle School is just that—a school. That means we are here to teach to those who wish to learn. The lead in that play had nothing in it to challenge you. It was all old hat for someone with your abilities. You would have learned nothing from the experience. But Marion Weinstein stands to learn a great deal from playing that part. She's a talented girl, but she doesn't have your experience."

He smiled ruefully. "Come, now, Maria. Surely you don't expect to get the lead in *every* school play?"

I grinned. "No, sir. And . . . thank you for explaining it."

Mr. Drew stood and put his hand on my shoulder. "There will be other plays. Other roles. Other leads. You will get some of them. But only the ones that I think will teach you something new." He grinned. "That's what acting's all about. Right?"

He was right.

And learning something new is what life's all about.

As I walked out of his office and down the hall to my pink locker, I grinned. Seventh grade was shaping up to be a very educational year.

"Maria!" I heard someone call out.

I turned and saw Evie hurrying toward me with a

large notebook. "May I ask you some questions?"

"Sure," I answered. "But what for?"

"Well," she answered quickly, "have you ever seen the *Best Friends* show on cable? It's really wild. Suddenly everyone's watching it. And it just kind of made me wonder how well the Unicorns know one another."

"You said yourself the Unicorns are the best friends in the world. Of course we know each other really well," I answered, shutting my locker and turning to lean on it. I looked across the hall at the bulletin board. There was a huge poster for a fund-raising bash sponsored by a group of eighth-grade girls called the Eight Times Eight Club. *Who are they?* I wondered. I made up my mind to find out.

Elizabeth tells the story of our next big adventure in The Unicorn Club #3, **THE BEST FRIEND GAME.** *Don't miss it!*

SIGN UP FOR THE SWEET VALLEY HIGH® FAN CLUB!

Hey, girls! Get all the gossip on Sweet Valley High's® most popular teenagers when you join our fantastic Fan Club! As a member, you'll get all of this really cool stuff:

- Membership Card with your own personal Fan Club ID number
- A Sweet Valley High® Secret Treasure Box
- Sweet Valley High® Stationery
- Official Fan Club Pencil (for secret note writing!)
- Three Bookmarks
- A "Members Only" Door Hanger
- Two Skeins of J. & P. Coats® Embroidery Floss with flower barrette instruction leaflet
- Two editions of *The Oracle* newsletter
- Plus exclusive Sweet Valley High® product offers, special savings, contests, and much more!

Be the first to find out what Jessica & Elizabeth Wakefield are up to by joining the Sweet Valley High® Fan Club for the one-year membership fee of only $6.25 each for U.S. residents, $8.25 for Canadian residents (U.S. currency). Includes shipping & handling.

Send a check or money order (do not send cash) made payable to "Sweet Valley High® Fan Club" along with this form to:

SWEET VALLEY HIGH® FAN CLUB, BOX 3919-B, SCHAUMBURG, IL 60168-3919

NAME_____
(Please print clearly)

ADDRESS_____

CITY_____ STATE_____ ZIP_____
(Required)

AGE_____ BIRTHDAY_____ /_____ /_____

Offer good while supplies last. Allow 6-8 weeks after check clearance for delivery. Addresses without ZIP codes cannot be honored. Offer good in USA & Canada only. Void where prohibited by law.
©1993 by Francine Pascal   LCI-1383-123